The Invasion That

Never Happened

By

Udi Menashe

The Invasion that Never Happened

Copyright © 2013 by Udi Menashe

Starfleet to Scoutship, please give your position, Over.
I'm in orbit around the third planet from the star called
the sun. Over.
You mean it's the Earth? Over.
Positive. It is known to have some form of intelligent
species. Over.
I think we should take a look.

"JIMI HENDRIX - THIRD STONE FROM THE SUN"

The Invasion that Never Happened

Printed and bound in the United States of America
First Edition
ISBN # 978-0-9968505-2-0

To my best friend Jeff Teitell.

A good man.

TABLE OF CONTENTS

Chapter 1 - Introduction

Do you remember the invasion that never happened? The 1970 alien invasion of California, USA? Yes, real walking, breathing, extra-terrestrial creatures from outer space. Do you remember this invasion? If you don't – have no worries. No one remembers or, at least, no one cares to remember. There must be a good reason for an unknown person to say, and I'll quote:

"If you can remember the sixties, then you weren't there"

And since we all know that 1970 wasn't that far from the sixties, on second thought, who can remember?

I, myself, don't remember much about this invasion, but if there is one thing I am sure about is that in the year 1970 in California, USA there was a full scale alien invasion. What made this invasion such forgettable event? How can anyone explain an alien army, who visited our planet not once but twice, and was unable to leave its mark behind? Not one shred of evidence of their attempt to take over our planet?

If there is any explanation it's that it really wasn't such a great invasion, but it wasn't the aliens' fault.

You see, in contrast to the invading aliens we're used to read about, the ones who underestimate our society and consider its population as easy prey, the 1970 aliens mistakenly overestimated us and for that reason approached us with extra caution. No matter the reason, one thing stands out; the 1970 alien invasion of California, USA wasn't a memorable event.

The aliens, for their part, didn't even try to disguise themselves. They were not covered head to toe with a complex shield, nor try to take on a human forms. Maybe, in the back of their very large heads, they hoped that their mere appearance would bring humanity to its knees. Well that didn't happen either as they were completely ignored by us. I can come up with a few really good reasons for that. We were busy, we were protesting, we were innovating – or maybe just because it was the sixties and we were stoned.

By now I'm sure that you are wondering what were the invading aliens looking for on planet Earth of 1970? After all, humans weren't that advanced, something that is not hard to prove. Follow the development of any creation of that time period, from computers to cars to toasters, only to comprehend the countless redo's we went through in our quest for perfection, not that we ever succeeded. Your first clue will be the toaster that even today is incapable of toasting a piece of bread evenly on both sides.

Well, in all fairness that's not entirely true. We did, though, had one thing the aliens were eager to own and willing to go as far as crossing galaxies and invading our planet. It was this one thing that in contrary to the rest of our creations, unfortunately, worsened with any of our attempts to improve it.

Yes, it was that special thing we call music, more specifically the music of the sixties, and even more specifically, it was the music of one man that we know as Jimi Hendrix.

I have no doubt that you remember Jimi. If you don't remember him or have never heard of him - know just this: Even today, more than forty years after his passing, Jimi Hendrix is still considered the greatest guitar player of all time. He was a talented American music artist who lived outside the USA and just happened to come back to his country during the "British Invasion." Yes, I do mean the same invasion that started in the early sixties and by 1970 was in full swing. Unfortunately for the aliens, it seems that the "British Invasion" did a pretty good job in eclipsing their invasion.

Jimi returned home and put on a show like we've never seen before. For god sake – he even burned his guitar on stage. He gave us the opportunity to recognize him for the musical genius he was, and we did. But amazing as it sounds, we weren't the only ones to recognize Jimi's creativity. Apparently, those purple creatures from a faraway galaxy did notice as well. For them, Jimi's music was a sufficient reason to invade our planet – but when they finally decided to act on it, we completely ignored them.

I'm sure that by now you are wondering about the link between Jimi Hendrix and the 1970 alien invasion that never happened. All I can tell you is that it was both Jimi and his music that played a major role in the aliens' invasion along with the events that transpired during the years he rose to fame. I know it sounds confusing, but be patient, there is a story here worth telling.

Without passing judgment on the generation of the late sixties and early seventies, I must admit that in my opinion, for them, the "British Invasion" had a much greater importance than the 1970 alien invasion. That might be just another reason how an invasion by a large alien army could pass completely unnoticed, like it never happened. For whatever reasons, it seems that in 1970, human priorities were all mixed up.

You see, they were standing on a crossroads and had to make a decision to either possess some really good, new, and amazing tunes or grab this once in a lifetime opportunity to acquire advanced alien technologies that would change theirs and our lives forever. And guess which they chose??

Is there any other way to rationalize how more than forty years down the road we own "smart" phones, with the most advanced stereo sound systems, while for the love of God, we still can't get decent voice reception on the same phones? Well now when I actually think about it, I must admit that most likely, I wouldn't have chosen any differently.

Maybe that in itself will help you understand how this full-scale alien invasion became an undetected incident. No one saw them when they came. No one was interested in their whereabouts and no one, for sure, saw them leave. As I said before - No one cared. If this invasion was ever documented as a "Wikipedia" entry, it would be listed under: "The 1970 alien invasion that never happened – See 'FAILURE'." If you came across this entry, you, most likely, would click your way to the term "FAILURE" – and guess what you'll find? "FAILURE – An attempt by an alien life form to invade planet Earth without enormous spaceships, ray guns or apparent set of plans, destined to go nowhere as they were completely ignored. P.S. Jimi Hendrix was in town performing."

Are you still wondering what involved this great musician, the most famous black, free-spirited person of all times, with extraterrestrial purple life forms?

What you should really wonder is this: What made these purple aliens, from another galaxy, become so infatuated with Jimi Hendrix and his music?

Well, that's a good question that comes with a great answer. You see, Jimi was a great believer in aliens and their existence. On more than one occasion, Jimi Hendrix even claimed to be an alien himself and while it didn't necessarily mean that he was one, it did indicate how he felt within the society in which he lived - alienated. You must understand that Jimi wasn't crazy. He just had a different point of view about aliens and their existence. All he was trying to tell us is that there was more than one way to live a life, more than one way to express yourself. Jimi wanted us to know that it is OK to live your life on your own terms, that you can be a borderline alien and that there is nothing wrong in being different. That for itself can be a good explanation why the aliens were so attracted to Jimi Hendrix.

It was Jimi who always stated:

"I'm the one that has to die when it's time for me to die, so let me live my life, the way I want to."

And in his short life he did just that, expressing himself through his incredible music, and his visual creativity reflected in his sartorial choices. If there was one thing Jimi gave us for safe keeping it was his music, which always had a captivating effect on us, humans and, for one or another unexplained reasons had the same captivating effect on the invading aliens. I can confirm that Jimi's music drew the aliens to Earth and was the main reason for this 1970 alien invasion that never happened.

The big mystery is how can it be that an alien nation from another galaxy was able to acquire access to Jimi Hendrix's music? There is no doubt that his music was divine, but still, it had to travel a great distance to reach their galaxy. Was Jimi Hendrix so talented that he was able to tune his guitar, point it at the sky and do the impossible: shoot his music through the stars, passing through time and place, and reaching the aliens? After all, an ordinary human can't do such a thing. Could it be that maybe, just maybe, Jimi wasn't an ordinary human? Could it be that he was really an alien?

The world will never know for sure, but we can speculate. Even today, there are those who believe that Jimi was an alien, an extraterrestrial being with such out-of-this-world qualities, which still reflected in the music he left behind. Truth to be told is that Jimi's music was always considered out-of-this-world.

There is even a story of a UFO sighting in Hawaii during Jimi's "Rainbow Bridge" concert on an extinct volcano in Maui. Calls were coming from all over the island of that sighting and like the rest of the island residents, Jimi witnessed the event. Now, what do you think was his reaction to that sight?

Well, Jimi just looked at the sky and told the crowd in his cool demeanor: *"There go my friends."* How cool is that?

Nevertheless, while it's true that Jimi was incredibly talented, this time he didn't point his guitar to the skies and release his music toward the aliens' colony. I am confident that if he wanted to do so it would be done with great success. But this 1970 alien invasion that never happened wasn't his doing. You can blame that one on us. We were the ones who increased their awareness of our planet and the human existence. More than that, we were the ones who indirectly introduced Jimi Hendrix and his music to the aliens, which ultimately made them invade our planet. Luckily, our society didn't make much sense to them and maybe for that reason I'm still here and able to tell you this tale. You can say that from the get go they just read us incorrectly and from that point on executed their invasion too cautiously. Even their initial approach of our planet was a kind of different.

Did I mention that this invasion started with a drop? Oh yes, a nontraditional way to start any invasion. It started with a drop and another drop and another drop. No spaceships, no weapons, and no big ray guns, just purple raindrops.

For millions of years the universe lived in overall tranquility. Galaxies were just floating beside galaxies, playing catch up with each other. But then came the sixties and we decided to join the game. Not to our knowledge, up till then, humans were under the aliens' radar. Compare us to something the aliens stored in their attics, never to be visited again. To the best of our knowledge, aliens had never landed on our planet before.

What about the 1947 Roswell incident, you ask? Well, it never happened either!! Ask any of those high-ranking Air Force generals and they'll firmly deny it, insisting it was nothing but a giant hot air balloon experiment gone wrong. They will tell you that all of the post-incident new technologies you see should be credited to a bunch of very smart humans and not to secret alien technology.

Now a high-ranking Air Force general wouldn't lie to us?!? Damn it! Does it mean that we need to figure out, all over again, who is really responsible for the pyramids in Egypt and Central America?

Regardless, when we joined the game we did it in style. You see, during the sixties we decided to take our space exploration aspirations more seriously and from there it was a very short distance to planet Earth's first and last full scale invasion by aliens. Yes, the 1970 alien invasion was a direct result of our space explorations, which inadvertently created an uncontrollable urge in the aliens' souls to come over and visit us. In my eyes they had a good reason. The aliens were desperate to listen to Jimi Hendrix's music. I'm sure that most likely, as with any other invading force, those aliens had some additional objectives on their agenda such as conquering and looting – but listening to Jimi's music was at the top of their list.

In the sixties' early years, humans developed this notion that instead of investing our funds and efforts in exploring our own blue and green planet, it be better to spend tenfold and build cool-looking rockets shaped like missiles. Following that we've decided to populate those rockets with highly trained humans who we called astronauts. We made sure that those good-looking astronauts be photogenic and capable to crack a smile to anyone with a camera. Obviously, we also trained those good-looking young men to handle those cool-looking rockets and fly them at full speed ahead into our new adventures in space. Only then came the most crucial part of this adventure, which was to find a cool name for this project, the kind of name that no one will object to or have problem to pronounce. So we spent around two hours and four minutes, flipped a coin three times and finally came up with that:

"The Space Exploration Program."

The name was very simple, but that space program was complex, made from a variety of space missions, all conceived by humans and almost all executed by them. Those missions were designed to explore any corner of outer space, we believed within the reach of our feet or hands. We had this crazy belief that it was our destiny not to leave one stone unturned in the vast space of the universe or, at a bare minimum, within the spectrum of our galaxy.

We started with unmanned missions, which we ran for the longest time and I'm positive that the only reason we ended those missions was out of boredom. We just couldn't communicate with any of the pilots of those unmanned rockets.

That moment of boredom marked the beginning of the more exciting space missions. It started with us sending a monkey on a mission, and immediately after we sent a dog into space. I'm almost positive that we even tried to send the monkey and the dog together on the next mission. This mission was a complete failure - they simply didn't like each other. But even this failure didn't pass without a good outcome. You see, we gave it a positive spin and took from it a very important lesson. We concluded that if a monkey and a dog who didn't like each other were able to find their way home, there was no reason that humans couldn't do the same. This was when we decided to send humans into space. This was the beginning of our manned missions.

Those missions were different and became bolder by the moment, going farther and farther in their attempts to invade the darkness of outer space. It started with simple orbit around planet Earth and moved to more elaborate missions around the moon. Finally, in 1969, we were able to land on the moon's surface and even left a flag and some few footprints behind as a proof.

Well, there is still some controversy about this moon landing mission and I don't mean whether this landing was real or not. You can check with any alien and he will confirm that there is, definitely, an American flag on the moon's surface. After all, any alien visiting Earth knows that he must use this flag as the last waypoint on his way to our planet.

His exact instructions is to make an immediate strong right turn as he pass that small rock with that red white and blue flag. Only then he should see planet Earth right in front of him. Should he miss the flag and the strong right turn, the alien must continue flying straight to the red planet, make a U-turn and try again.

The real moon landing's controversy was about something else altogether. Where did we exactly landed? Did we land on the dark side of the moon or on the moon's other side on a really dark day?

All in all, our space missions were very well planned and calculated. They all had an exact time of departure, as long as we were able to be exact. There was a calculated time to spend in outer space and a précised scheduled time of return, which, unfortunately, during the early stages of our space exploration wasn't exact and in more than one occasions never met at all.

Our next step was to collect a group of great humans, scientists to be specific, to follow those missions or, more accurate, to scrutinize them. We situated them in a big dark room filled with lots of cool machines, the kind that equipped with lights and buttons and full of mysterious squawking sounds. This was a very serious group of humans, especially as they were spending hours sitting in this big dark room, staring at those lights, pressing all those buttons and listening to all of those mysterious sounds. They never crack a smile. But should one of them suddenly say: *"We have a Touchdown."* Oh man, that would be a completely different story. Their mood would immediately change and they would cheer and smile with no end in sight. I've never understood why.

This is the best way to describe our very serious space exploration program and its very serious missions during the sixties, in a nut shell. Now, in contrast to those very calculated missions we also had some other missions, which we don't mention much. Those were the missions we cared much less about or maybe even didn't care at all.

You see, right after the monkey and dog incident as our space exploration program progressed and moved forward, we became cocky and a crazy new idea was born. We started to think how cool it would be to send our stuff into the deeper part of outer space, that one place we couldn't go ourselves? I guess the way we perceived it was that if we couldn't get there, at least our stuff would.

This crazy idea, which we believed to be a bright idea, led to the development of something new that we called the "Time Capsule."

To describe it, think about a large storage device, shaped like a barrel and a cone-shaped head glued together. It also had a very smart lock, which was made to be opened by a life form with basic intelligence. It had to be intelligent enough to solve the smart lock riddle: "2+2 equals what?" You see, we had to be sure that whoever came across those "Time Capsules" had to be at least as smart as us. Can you see any other reason for such complex security device? None I can think of other than the chance that some lonely people on Earth were hoping to meet new friends, someone intelligent and maybe even exciting.

Our official justification for the whole "Time Capsule" deal was that it was our way of introducing ourselves to whoever was out there in the deeper part of outer space. Off the record, I will tell you that it was our way to signal to whoever is out there in the deeper part of outer space: "Look what we have and you don't."

As you all know, since the beginning of time and throughout human history, "Showoff" was always an important component of our existence, and in the sixties, it wasn't any different.

So it happened that every so often, in between our vital space missions, we blasted into outer space one of those "Time Capsules," filled with the most glorified showoff items we were able to collect on Earth. Due to a size limitation, we had no choice but to stuff them with any Earth goodie that just might fit and left some of our coolest items behind. I am convinced that if those "Time Capsules" were more spacious, you would see a real life-size 1965, red "Ford Mustang" convertible rolling into one of them on its way to outer space. Since that wasn't possible, instead we made sure to pack an exact miniature replica of the same car in its original packaging and even glued a sticky note to its packaging saying "In order to keep in mint condition – DO NOT OPEN!!"

Chapter 2 – The "Time Capsule" Incident

We were moving forward, blasting those "Time Capsules" into space, but since humans are not that ambitious, we've never tried to send them beyond the "limited" range of our galaxy. Being so unmotivated, it never crossed our minds to make a life forms in other galaxies, other than ours, jealous of us. You see, we were concentrating all our efforts to find any alien life form that might exist in our own galaxy. We were sure that finding even a single one and making it jealous of us would be satisfying enough.

But then in the beginning of 1967, something we didn't plan happened, an unexpected freak accident that transpired with no intervention on our part. We lost one of those "Time Capsules." It was in route to Alpha Centauri, one of the brightest stars in our galaxy, and suddenly disappeared off our radars, causing some of those serious humans in that big dark room to age overnight. Unknowingly to us, this "Time Capsule" flew to close to a passing Wormhole and was dragged into it by its gravity force. The only thing we knew was that it disappeared for good.

It was sucked into the Wormhole's entrance and slid through it at an accelerated speed reaching its other end, the one we normally call "The Exit." Passing through the Wormhole, it reached our neighboring galaxy, a small purple galaxy that was occupied by the same alien nation who ultimately invaded our planet in 1970.

Well, to be more accurate, it didn't exactly reached them but more likely spit out of the wormhole at a ferocious speed on a collision course with one of their spaceships that just happened to be passing by. That encounter caused a substantial damage to the aliens' vessel, knocking off its left-side mirror and causing cosmetic damage to the spaceship's shiny metallic paint from front to back.

The aliens inside the spaceship were rattled. Since their intergalactic weather forecast channel had no forecast of any meteor showers in their area, they assume that they were under attack and immediately raised their spaceship's shields and scanned their surroundings. There was nothing out there but a weird-shaped item, floating alongside their spaceship. For the aliens it looked like a barrel and a cone that were glued together with a large rectangle-shaped emblem on the barrel side and a kind of funny lock. They gave the emblem a closer look. It was red, white and blue with some stripes and something that resembled stars, not the kind of stars they were accustomed to, but more like ones that had been drawn by an untalented four-year-old alien child.

After another thorough scan, the aliens took a deep breath and slowly lowered their shields. They scooped up the weird-shaped object and took it to their home planet hoping that a closer inspection might reveal its owner's identity. They knew that finding the object's owner was crucial if they wished to receive compensation for the cosmetic damage and broken left mirror they had just lost.

Being an intelligent life form, they soon solved the smart lock riddle and opened the "Time Capsule." One short glance into the device belly and its content was sufficient for them to lose any shred of hope for monetary compensation. The content was useless, like a primitive technology that was dumped by its owners who from one damn reason decided to use their galaxy as a land fill.

Still, out of curiosity, they started to go through the "Time Capsule" content, inspecting each of the items slightly and tossing them aside. For them, our 1967 items were rough in design and hard on the eyes. They didn't even take a second look at the Ford "Mustang" replica and its attached note as their claws ripped the packaging into shreds before it was tossed to the room's corner along with the rest of the discarded items.

During the process, one of the aliens stretched out his arm into the "Time Capsule" belly and grabbed the next item. It was one of Earth's newest inventions, one of our latest toys, our pride and joy, a Radio Shack 1962 Tape Cassette Recorder/Player. Since we were so proud of this device, it was able to make the short list in our "showoff" items and found its place inside the "Time Capsule." But as proud as we were of this device, we were even prouder of its content, the actual cassette inside it. Well, it wasn't the actual cassette we were so proud about, but the recording in it.

This recording wasn't anything like you can envision. It wasn't a message of peace from our president to whoever was out there and it wasn't even a welcoming message, made from a set of calculated sounds produced by our scientists. It was a music recording. Oh yes, we were so proud of that piece of music that we were willing to send it to outer space. After all, it was the music of 1967 Earth's newly rising star, the greatest guitar player of all times, Jimi Hendrix. Now you tell me, how is that for showing off?

The aliens were no more interested in this device than they were in the rest of the "Time Capsule" items. The alien inspected the tape for a brief moment and was about to toss it aside onto the growing pile of discarded items in the room's corner when, completely by chance, his claw got caught between the device's buttons. He found himself shaking his arm in all directions, trying to release his claws and get as far as he could from that dreadful device. Doing so, the "PLAY" button got pressed and the device's red light turned on. You could hear the Tape Player's familiar static sound, an expected sound from a 1962 audio device, something that made the aliens freeze in their tracks. Listening to this static sound, they stared at each other, not exactly sure what they were listening to when, suddenly, Jimi's magical music started playing.

The magic filled the room and caught the aliens off guard. There was nothing they could do to shield themselves, something I can confirm from personal experience. Jimi Hendrix's music have always had the same effect on me. And now the same captivating tunes grabbed the aliens' souls and didn't let go. Now as time and everything around them just froze, they stopped their doing, sat down, closed their metallic eyes and let the music carry them to faraway galaxies, to places they had never been before or even imagined that ever existed. Well this is the most common reaction to Jimi Hendrix's music.

When the cassette reached its end, the aliens played it again, cranking the device volume to its highest level. Now, the loud music was able to leave that small room and reached the structure's remote areas, drawing additional aliens to it. A few moments of exposure, and those aliens were hooked too. Up to now there had been no apparent explanation for the magical effect Jimi's music had on those aliens, but regardless it was that moment, when the aliens were introduced to his music. It was the same moment that started the chain of events, which would lead them to our planet in the invasion that never happened.

Oh yes, all the aliens in the room were immediately hooked on Jimi's music to the point of addiction. A short time after, they realized that there was an urgent matter to deal with. There was something they had to do about this addiction as soon as they could. And they did. Without losing a moment, the aliens attached our Earthly device to their colony's emergency audio system. As a result, across their colony, all the aliens were able to enjoy the same divine music, which obviously was playing continuously.

As you might guess, now there was a whole alien nation in a faraway purple galaxy that was hooked on Jimi Hendrix's music, which was playing around-the clock.

You must understand what made the aliens so enchanted with Jimi's music. You see, here on Earth it was Jimi's music and his rapturous, masterful guitar playing that attracted us, but with the aliens it was much deeper than that. Like us, they were listening to the same music, but were able to hear something additional that couldn't be heard by us. It was something that made sense to them, a hidden message about life and its goodness. It was that pure message that drew them to Jimi and his music to the point of addiction.

The human made device kept playing for days until the inevitable happened. The batteries became completely drained. It started with signs of sound distortion followed by the flickering of the red power light. Slowly the music started to fade out and then, without notice, the music stopped all together and the tape player red power light died.

Needless to say, it was a devastating moment that caught the aliens by surprise. By now they were addicted to Jimi's music and this unfortunate curve ball compelled them back to the humans' device for a second and much closer inspection. The aliens turned the tape player in all directions, inspecting each and every side of the small device, only to discover a hidden compartment at its base. It was a small compartment, hidden behind a small, hard plastic door that was flushed with the device's body and attached with a small metal circle, marked with a cross on its head. That discovery made the aliens wonder why the device designer created such covert compartment. What was this compartment hiding? Was this the answer for the device's lack of functionality? The aliens were curious of that hidden compartment's content.

Unknown to the aliens that little metal part with the cross on its head was a simple "Philips Head" screw. Since they've never encountered such complex item, the aliens immediately summoned their strongest alien to pry open that mysteries compartment. That alien flexed his muscles, grabbed the device and disjointed the small door from the device's body, letting four barrel-shaped metallic items to pop out and roll across the metallic surface. Not knowing what those parts were, the aliens scrutinized them and found the marking: "Double AA." The aliens have just stumble upon the tape player's batteries.

At first, they couldn't figure out what the batteries were, but soon deduced these were the device's power source. They assumed that in order to revive the device and play the captivating music again, they would have to replace those four power sources with new ones of the same kind. That assumption led them to a simple conclusion. Since they couldn't survive without the music, it was essential for them to obtain new small power sources of the same kind, four at a bare minimum. And since those items were nowhere to be found on their planet, they would have to initiate a search, a quest to find replacement "Double AA" batteries. Still they were completely lost of where to start their search.

So they decided to inspect the four little power sources one more time looking for additional markings only to find one additional marking that caught their eyes. It was on a separate line made out of four words. It was that crucial sentence that drew the aliens to our planet:

"Made in California, USA."

The aliens realized that if there was a place that held the key for the strange small power sources, the replacement "Double AA" batteries, it was a place that went by the name: California, USA.

Since this alien nation was always spontaneous, they never contemplated too much in a time of crisis and always made sure to find solutions on the fly. This was a time of crisis, and the aliens decided to apply the same kind of logic to the drained batteries situation. They had an urgent need to replace these used up power sources, the drained batteries. Those batteries were in a place named California, USA and that for itself left them with no other choice but to go to California, USA and one way or another, get those replacement "Double AA" batteries.

Simply saying, the way they saw it, they had no other option, but to invade California, USA.

They had it all figured out. They were able to identify the problem at hand, realize the source of the problem, and even come very quickly to a solution to their problem. One might say that they were very proud with themselves.

But now, when everything was said and done, there was one small detail for them to figure out...

Where in the hell was California, USA?

Yes, it was a small, but very important detail. The aliens felt depleted, set quietly and wondered what to do next. While they were pondering their next step, one of the aliens' eyes wandered to the "Time Capsule" and the weird-looking rectangular-shaped emblem that was glued to its side. As he was speculating what artist would draw such an immature emblem in red, white, and blue with stripes and stars that looked like they were drawn by a four-year-old, untalented alien child, he had an idea.

Why don't they send an image of this emblem to all of their neighbors and see if, maybe, they can make sense of that amateur artist's origin, which most likely would reveal the source of the playing device.

It was a simple and great idea that the aliens decided to execute. They rushed around and contacted all of their neighbors, sending them a copy of this emblem, with a simple question: "Have you seen this before?"

Shortly after, to their surprise, they were contacted by one of their neighbors with an affirmative answer, telling them they had encountered that same exact emblem on more than one occasions. Their neighbors told them that in the nearby galaxy, the one that resembled spilled white liquid; there was a small vacant rock that spun aimlessly, like a fly, around a larger planet, colored blue and green. In their neighbors' opinion, there was someone on the bigger planet who was definitely annoyed by this little rock as he had been trying, for years, to shoot it down. That someone even went as far as continuously launching large rockets toward that small vacant rock, only to miss it each and every time. Their neighbors added that most of those large rockets had the same red, white, and blue emblem glued to their side.

This news cheered the aliens and with renewed hope, they contacted their neighbors once again, inquiring if they could shed a light on the meaning of that place, named "California, USA." This time, their neighbors' response was even more surprising and came in a form of a small package, a metal case, which included aerial maps, tourist brochures and scenery postcards of the state of California. The aliens inspected the material and were surprised to find a small note, dated 1947, on the back side of the beautiful postcards. It was written in the alien language: *"We are OK, still here and having fun."*

That finding enhanced their feeling of security. They were happy to know that our planet could be penetrated or invaded by aliens.

But it wasn't that simple. Their neighbors warned them to be careful with the inhabitants of this blue and green planet, the ones they called humans. They remind them that only a reckless, irresponsible society would randomly shoot such large rockets towards a small, vacant and harmless rock, no matter how annoying it was.

As much as the aliens appreciated their neighbors' warning and took it into heart, they knew that there was no other choice, but to invade. As a token of gratitude, the aliens sent their neighbors a gift basket, loaded with their planet's night crawler delicacy and a "Thank You" note with a hand-drawn picture of a purple alien head with a big smile.

Now they had better knowledge of their target, California USA. The aliens actually used the same tourist postcards to choose their exact targets in California, the two cities to invade, and it wasn't a hard choice. Those were the two cities that were best portrayed in those postcards, the cities of Los Angeles and San Francisco.

Based on their neighbors' stern warning, they decided to initiate a scouting mission into the two cities prior of their invasion. They had to gather information about the nature of the reckless human society and the exact location of their magical "Double AA" power sources. Above all, they were also hoping that their scouts might trace the same entity who created this magical music, the human who went by the name of Jimi Hendrix. The drained batteries issue was of a high urgency and the aliens had no time to waste. They would move ahead, quickly, with their scouting mission and send two small scouting teams to California, USA, one for each city.

Now think about it, when you make a rush decision to invade someone else's planet with a primary objective of obtaining "Double AA" batteries, you putting yourself in a very special place in history. It is that place, where no one will ever question why your full-scale invasion failed so miserably, and that applies to our aliens. It seems as they rushed into this adventure with no meticulous planning and, worse of all, with no plan B, the same one we call the "Just in Case" plan. It seems that their invasion was doomed to fail

There were one or more reasons that it could fail. It could be the lack of enormous spaceships. It might be the absence of the side arms or maybe, just maybe, it would be the language barrier that failed them, their inability to communicate with us. After all, intimidating large spaceships, scary ray guns, and communication skills are the bare essentials for any alien invasion. And it seems that our aliens had none of those.

But let me clarify, that wasn't the case of with our aliens, they were not supposed to fail. They had enormous spaceships and large ray guns and even had a grasp of the English language. More than that - all of those components were incorporated into a calculated and meticulous invasion plan. It wasn't supposed to be like that, but it did only for a very small and unexpected detail. The aliens couldn't imagine that they would be ignored by us, something that made their invasion go completely unnoticed, like it never happened.

In my view, this failure could be attributed to the aliens' choice of time and place. After all, they decided to invade two of California's largest cities right at the end of a very strange time period, the sixties. It was that time period were those two cities played a major role in shaping our society future. The cities of Los Angeles and San Francisco were the cradle for the counterculture and civil right movements that sprung up during the turbulent times of the Vietnam War, something that was unknown to the aliens. For them, those cities must have had a great importance for another reason as they were listed on one of the brochures they received from their neighbors. It was the same brochure that carried the image and name of the human who had created their beloved music, a brochure that listed Jimi Hendrix' scheduled tours in 1970.

How could they miss the opportunity to visit those cities and see Jimi performing on stage? The aliens wouldn't dream of missing such an opportunity so they decided to construct their full-scale invasion plans around Jimi Hendrix's tour schedule of 1970.

At the same time that they were figuring their future invasion plans, the aliens started preparing for their scouting mission of the two large metropolises. Later they'll argue to make choose correctly, but I beg to differ. Not being a military genius, I'm certain that if the aliens spent some time visiting one of Earth's bookstores, reading our best Sci-Fi novels, their invasion outcome would have turned out differently. If they went through Earth's greatest Sci-Fi novels, written by Earth's greatest Sci-Fi story tellers, maybe then we could remember this invasion that never happened.

Little to be known, our Sci-Fi novels can shed light on other alien invasions throughout human history. Those books could have given the aliens the blueprints for any successful imaginary alien invasion of our planet throughout our existence. If the aliens read through them, preferably while sipping a cup of java in one of our small coffee shops, located in one of the big cities' street corners, they would come to the same conclusion we reached a long time ago.

You see, alien invasions of Earth are usually destined to fail and the few that succeeded were mainly because of one major trait.

A successful alien invasion always transpires in Earth's most rural places. It is true. Alien invasions were always better off on Earths' most remote locations, the ones occupied by friendly farmers. Those are the places populated with humans who are willing to accept any stranger with open arms, no questions asked, while offering him a piece of their wife's fresh-baked apple pie. As much as it sound as an appealing concept, what really made those rural areas perfect for any invasion?

Well, there are a few rationales. First and foremost, those areas are best known for their large open fields. The same large fields that accommodated the farmers' harvest day picnics can easily transformed into a perfect parking space for a large alien spaceship fleet of any amount, size, and shape.

Then there is the isolation factor, which turns the rural areas into the finest gathering spot of any invading alien force. Landing in an isolated location, hidden from the local residents' curiosity, the invading forces can assemble their equipment without interruptions while sipping their alien juice and relieving themselves from the long journey to our planet.

Lastly I must tell you about the rural areas' residents. Being so isolated from society increases their craving for new information from any outsider, human or alien, which ultimately makes them an easy target. They are very accommodating, willing to listen to any story, especially the ones that don't involve livestock, bowel movements or burning crosses in the middle of the night, a phenomenon that was very popular everywhere in the rural areas during the sixties. The locals need for information, enhancing their acceptance while reducing their suspicion of any passing stranger, even those in the form of an invading alien army that just landed on Billy Bob's corn field.

Earth's Sci-Fi novels went on to describe the second stage of any imaginary alien invasion in our rural areas, bringing to light the most exciting advantages those areas offered to an invading alien force, something that might have worked great for our aliens.

You may not know, but aliens are great jokers and always enjoy the mystery their sightings install in us. Is there any other explanation for all those "Almost Encounters" we hear about? You see, there is nothing better for aliens than to bother a naïve, church-going farmer in the middle of the night. This is the main reason why any second stage in an imaginary alien invasion involves unexplained hovering sounds, bright lights and a lot of "Whoosh" metallic commotion that normally start after midnight. All of this usually transpires right above the sleeping farmer and his wife's bedroom and will finish with a grand finale that involves missing cattle and highly irritated, red-eyed farmers, suffering from major sleep deprivation.

Yes, this is the obvious second stage of any successful imaginary alien invasion and fortunately for us, that wasn't the case in the 1970 alien invasion that never happened. In fact our aliens didn't spend any money to purchase or time to read Earth's Sci-Fi novels in one of our small coffee shops on our street corners. Instead they designed their invasion plans with a completely different course of action, deciding to dispatch two scouting teams to the two large metropolises, three years ahead of their planned invasion.

It's my opinion that their dismissal of the promising rural areas and bold decision to invade California's two large cities was a grave mistake on their part. The simple fact is that they were not ready just yet to join the big league – or in other words, the aliens were not mentally equipped to deal with us, city people.

Yes, the aliens were big jokers, but dealing with city people is not a joking matter. When an alien even slightly considers invading a major metropolis, he should also take into consideration if he is up for the task. I don't believe they understood or had a clue how different the big city rules of engagement were from the ones of the rural areas, and I'll explain.

For starters, it is a mandatory requirement for any invading forces to establish a channel of communication with the local population. Unlike the rural areas, with its small scattered population, in an over-populated major metropolis any contact with the local population demands large amounts of resources, supplies and foot soldiers, something that becomes a logistical nightmare. The aliens will find themselves exposed to the ongoing bickering of the needy local population while in the rural areas they can handle the same process at a much slower pace on a "one on one" basis.

In a teeming metropolis, it is imperative for the aliens to have the ability to converse with the local population at the time of the invasion. After all, they need to handle crowd control, issue orders, and most importantly, get the locals' help in navigating through the big city's complex streets. If you don't know, aliens always lose their way in those cities and find themselves in constant need of help to reach their next destination, or as they prefer to call it - their next target.

But city folks are not that accommodating, especially when you compare them to the nice folks in the rural areas. It is a given that the invading alien forces will lose their way in the web-like streets of a large metropolis and that would lead to crucial time delays that would affect the whole invasion progress. Big city residents are always busy with their affairs and less willing to lend a hand to strangers with a funny accent or to a lost alien army, especially, the kind that approaches you with their invasion maps in hand and ask you for directions to their next target.

Any military operation planner will tell you outright – there is nothing worse than to lose your way in a large metropolis at the height of an invasion for any invading force, including an alien force. Should the aliens find a local resident kind enough to help them, he or she most probably and with no bad intentions, would provide them with the wrong directions. As a result the aliens will find themselves lost at the late hours of the night in the most dangerous part of town. And as we all know, it will turn the hunter into the hunted and they will be lucky to escape those areas with their shirts on their backs.

Now you can see how an alien nation that chose to invade not one, but two of our largest municipalities was able to seal its fate and at the same time exponentially increased its troubles. A simple mathematical equation can easily prove how, at a bare minimum, the aliens just doubled their probability to get lost in the cities' maze and find themselves late at night in the most dangerous part of town. The only thing I can hope is that the aliens brought with them a change of clothing.

Spending just a short time in our big cities, among us, will teach the invading aliens an important lesson about us, city people. It is close to impossible for anyone and I do mean anyone to convince us to submit to their demands or for that matter that our lives are in grave danger. Big city residents are already aware that the mere idea of living in a large town represents their acceptance to put their lives in constant danger. In other words, you can say that by choosing to live in a major metropolis, we make the conscious decision to risk our lives with every step we take. How many times has your life hung on a thread while trying to cross a major intersection on your way to, let's say, a demonstration or a public gathering, which were two of the most common activities of the sixties? Now, try to imagine what might have happened if you were attempting to help a suspicious elderly lady to cross the same cross streets. Surprisingly, suspicious elderly ladies are fast to react while aroused, and always carry big purses with hard and heavy items.

Those are only some of the large metropolis obstacles, but if there is one thing that tops it all, it would be the large cities parking issues. It is a well-known matter in any big city, ask any human. It is horrible, disastrous, and impossible, especially, when your vehicle of choice is an oversized spaceship. Big cities are overcrowded with automobiles and parking spaces are always in scarce supply. Finding a decent parking spot can be a tedious task and a major headache to any car owner. Multiply it by ten when you're riding an oversized spaceship, a machine of war larger than a regular-size automobile.

There is no question that a decent parking space is in the eye of the beholder, but what we consider a great parking space might be seen by an alien as an unfit parking spot for his latest and shiniest spaceship. I am talking about the latest model spaceship, the kind that comes with a great lease option of zero down and payments spread over a hundred years, with an easy buy-back. Those type of aliens are always over-concerned of their spaceships' exterior and carry its sun cover wherever they go to protect it from the brutal sun, dust, and passing birds that ate the wrong worm. Consider those types of aliens with their shiny spaceships and combine it with the large cities parking issues and you will see the creation of a new nightmare for any invading alien army. That, in itself, will hit a cord in their souls and flood them with nostalgia of the inviting, open fields of Earth's rural areas, a memory so vivid that they won't even need to close their eyes to relive the beautiful crop circles they left behind.

In summary, rural area invasion is very simple: find an empty crop field, preferably a cornfield; land your spaceships and start making cattle disappear. Annoy the local farmers out of their minds and be sure to disappear into thin air with a clean getaway as you recognize that the local population has overcome its initial fear (which normally happens when you see them assembling in the city hall). P.S. – don't forget to leave behind some of those famous crop circles.

On the other hand, large metropolitan invasions are complicated from the get go. The rude local population will never submit to your demands or be courteous enough to move their vehicles and clear parking spaces for the invading spaceships. Even if they do, they will never leave enough spare time in the parking meters. This is a big problem for invading aliens who have just landed and not in possession of the local currency. There is no good outcome to any invasion, which starts with parking citations. To avoid those citations, an alien must hover, sometimes for days, above a metropolis and beg the humans below to keep enough free time in those parking meters. Unfortunately, owing to the language barrier, those pleas will fall on deaf ears.

Have you ever looked at the clear night skies and seen a shiny bright light moving erratically in all directions? Well, you were witnessing an alien spaceship doing its best, with no success I might add, to find a decent parking space.

Nevertheless, our aliens were forging ahead with their unusual plans to invade the cities of Los Angeles and San Francisco in a desperate search for replacement "Double AA" batteries. And those plans were unusual, especially, when I tell you about the aliens' method of arrival, the way they set foot on our planet. Did I mention before that this alien invasion started with a drop? Are you wondering what does it means to start an invasion with a drop? Well, it means that the aliens found a way to approach our planet unnoticed and by doing so, chose a very untraditional method.

The aliens decided to invade our planet without their large spaceships, ray guns or even the use of major explosions. They left it all behind in outer space and had their reasons. Instead, they touched down on our planet surface as drops, and I do mean, literally, drops. This invasion started with a single drop, and then another drop and another and another...

As farfetched as it sounds in their attempt to keep the element of surprise, they came as a rain, made of little aliens' drops. One might say that the aliens literally dropped in. If your imagination just created a picture of very large drops, each big enough to contain a single alien, you will need to work on your imagination. You see, the aliens were not that tiny and it would call for very large, even enormous drops. Such drops would, definitely, be noticed by us and most likely will hurt some innocent humans down below in the process.

The drops I'm talking about were the size of a normal rain drop, but with one exception. These drops were dark purple and had a very specific purpose, to be collected and reassembled again into aliens. To be more accurate, each of the incoming aliens had to be gathered and reassembled again from a total of 10,473 individual dark purple drops – that's a lot of drops.

I know, it sounds like somewhat of a sophisticated method to make an entrance. After all, it is one of the most advanced transport methods I've ever heard of, ranking only second to the beaming method we've become accustomed to from the show "Star Trek" (which was never proven to be workable anyway – at least, outside of "Star Trek").

But sophisticated as it might sound, this process had a major downside, which the aliens were not aware of until it was too late. It proved itself to be an excruciatingly slow and tremendously boring method that almost made the invading aliens lose their minds in the process. And even if they didn't lose their minds, there is no question that they definitely lost the element of surprise and the local population's interest in their invasion. I know it sounds unreal, but this slow and boring drop process, the aliens' method of transportation to Earth, did happen.

But we are getting ahead of ourselves as I haven't told you yet about the aliens' scouting mission, the one that came three years before their 1970 invasion that never happened.

Chapter 3 – The Scouting Mission

Let's get back to our story. Right after the "Time Capsule" incident, the aliens became concerned about what their neighbors called "The human society," which they had never heard of and introduced to in such an unpleasant way. They were wondering, what kind of reckless society just shoots stuff into outer space with no consideration for the rest of the universe and without advanced notice? What kind of life form has such disregard for its neighbors, even the ones in a faraway galaxy that can only be reached by chance via a passing wormhole that just happened to be in the area?

Regardless of their concerns, the urgent need for the primitive device power sources made it imperative for them to initiate a scouting mission of that reckless society. They had to do so to prepare for a future full scale invasion, and if nothing else, to figure out planet Earth's residents. Most importantly they had to trace the exact location of those precious "Double AA" batteries. The aliens had to gain knowledge about our society, but at the same time hoped their scouts would be resourceful enough to acquire the replacement batteries and eliminate the need of a full-blown, expensive invasion.

And so it happened. In 1967, three years prior to their planned invasion, our planet was scouted by two alien teams, each equipped with one of the four drained batteries that were so treasured by the aliens. Even as those drained "Double AA" batteries were their prize possession, the aliens knew that the scouts would need them as a prototype in their quest for new ones. The aliens made sure to keep the other two batteries on their home planet, encased in a bell-shaped glass that was placed in their main square for everyone to see and remember the great wonders of these tiny devices that gave rise to the exquisite sounds emitted from the device they had discovered. It also served as a notice to the aliens, to never forget how urgent it was to obtain an endless supply of these power source units, the replacement batteries, no matter what it took.

The scouts' mission was set for a six-month time frame with an optional six months extension. The two teams were to transport to Earth's surface using a single spaceship. As they reached their first stop, Los Angeles, the pilot would unload one team and continue immediately to his second drop location in San Francisco. Only then would the pilot park the spaceship in an undisclosed location, a place that wouldn't attract attention. His exact instructions were to park and wait for the duration of the mission, six-months with an optional six month extension, to retrieve the two scouting teams for their journey back home.

The scouting mission had two objectives: to merge with the local population and to obtain replacement "Double AA" batteries, if possible. The first objective's purpose was to study human habits and flaws, to gain knowledge about our society and figure out a means of communication with us. The aliens wanted to use this information to their advantage at the time of the invasion. At a bare minimum they had to master the basics of our language, the commands to apply at the time of our planet's invasion, the bare essential commands for any invasion. The aliens had to know how to say things like: "Hands Up", "Lay on the Floor" and "Can you, please, move your car so I can park my spaceship?"

They believed the more information they acquired about human behavior and their language could only help the invaders force the invaded to submit to their demands. Well, I do agree the aliens had the right to believe in whatever they wanted to, but I'm also sure they never met such a self-centered society as ours. I guess there is always the first time for everything.

The second objective, to attempt secure a new stock of replacement batteries, had a higher urgency. The scouts were instructed to put their hands – or in their case, their claws – on as many "Double AA" batteries as possible, even a four pack. Sitting in the briefing room, before their departure, their supervisor instructed them in a very direct manner to use any means at their disposal to obtain the highly desired Tape Player power source units, i.e., the batteries. He specifically spelled it out to them that "any means possible" meant even to go as far as purchasing the items at an inflated cost, if necessary.

The supervisor's briefing ended, and the scouts boarded the spaceship that would take them on their mission to Earth. The pilot sealed the spaceship's doors and lifted off. He started the long journey to their destination, making his way to the wormhole. The spaceship reached its entrance and zipped through it, sliding and turning wildly, crossing galaxies to its other side. Reaching our Milky Way galaxy, the pilot adjusted his bearing and cautiously merged onto one of the galaxy's highways. He maneuvered the spaceship toward our solar system's coordinates. And when the spaceship inched closer to our solar system, the pilot reduced the spaceship's speed.

Now he started using the charts the aliens received from their neighbors. He was tracing the planets in our solar system, by size and color. The pilot flew gently, maneuvering the spaceship toward the blue and green planet, slowly reaching the small vacant rock that was spinning aimlessly around it and made an immediate strong right turn as he passed it. The pilot and his passengers took a deep breath; in front of them lay their final destination, planet Earth.

The spaceship was about to initiate the most crucial part of their mission, the approach to our planet and landing on its surface.

The pilot was quiet as he guided the spaceship into Earth's atmosphere, crossing through it quickly, zipping toward the Pacific Ocean. The shiny spaceship hovered smoothly above the Pacific Ocean's cold water as it was approaching the United States' west coast and the state of California. Everyone on board was quiet. They knew that they had just passed the point of no return. The hunt for the replacement power sources, the "Double AA" batteries, was on.

Up till that point it seemed as if everything was going as planned. The long journey to our planet, the wormhole crossing, the entrance into Earth's atmosphere and the approach to California's shores went without a hitch. The scouts moved around the small spaceship, gearing up for their mission. They were calm, believing that there was no reason for anything to go awry – but they were dead wrong. The aliens were just about to encounter the first hiccup of their scouting mission.

You see, although it seems that the aliens invested an ample amount of time to carefully select the best two cities, in their opinion, to invade, it seems they spent no time selecting the best landing sites in those cities. And I do mean the two neighborhoods that would serve as the scout teams' drop locations – Earth's ground zero. Those would be the two locations that will find their place in the aliens' history articles as the places of "First Contact" between the aliens and the human society.

Not that there was anything wrong with the two chosen neighborhoods. After all, those neighborhoods were populated by humans, but let's just say that those neighborhoods were not, exactly, the best representation of the two cities' general population or of the State of California or of the USA or for that matter of Earth itself.

It started when the spaceship was about to reach its assigned first drop location in Los Angeles. The pilot approached the city under the darkness of the Pacific Ocean only to be suddenly flooded by the bright lights of the "City of angels." He was doing his best, with great success, to merge the spaceship's glowing lights with the ones below. The spaceship was gliding quietly above the city, reaching the marked drop location and then it happened. The pilot couldn't find parking. Instead, he found himself circling, for two whole days, above the city skies, searching for an empty parking space. The scouts did their best to help him. They were spotting and pointing him toward available parking spots, but as the pilot rushed to that empty spot and attempted to land, it would be taken by a human automobile.

And so it happened in 1967, for a period of two days, above the lighted skies of Los Angeles, there were countless reports of UFO sightings by the city residents. All reports were the same – erratic, uncontrolled lights moving left and right, up and down across the city skies with no apparent purpose. By the end of the second day the pilot managed to track an empty spot, sufficient enough for his spaceship. He made a dash for it, hovered above it for a few seconds, unable to believe that it was still available, and only then gently landed the spaceship.

Post landing, he sat quietly for a few minutes, winding down from the unexpected ordeal; and then started the spaceship shutdown procedure. He was shutting down the spaceship engines, prior to opening its hatch to release the first scouting team.

He didn't even kill the engines' secondary switches when, out of nowhere, the spaceship was flooded from behind with flashing red and blue lights. Followed those lights came a sharp loud voice over a speaker, instructing the pilot to immediately remove his vehicle from the grassy area, which wasn't intended to serve as a parking space. The voice continued, saying that a failure to comply would result in a citation, a court appearance and – in some extreme cases – an all-expense paid vacation in the county jail – courtesy of the Los Angeles Police Department.

The pilot had mixed feelings to the flashing lights and the sharp loud voice. On one hand, despite the fact that he didn't understand one word, he couldn't ignore the commanding tone, the sound of authority. On the other hand, it was disturbing for him to encounter such commanding entity on his first contact with the human society. What would be his nation's army experience, at the time of the invasion, if all humans were that commanding? Still, he felt content when he was able to associate the colorful flashing lights with the colors of the emblem that was glued to the "Time Capsule." He knew for sure that he had reached his target - California, USA.

The pilot couldn't care less about any interaction with the commanding voice and decided to save that whole "First Contact" mumble-jumble to the members of the Los Angeles scout team. His next action was to, practically, kick the confused team out of the spaceship, with no hugs, goodbyes or good luck. He then sealed the spaceship hatch, put the spaceship in forward position and took off into the dark skies as fast has he could without looking back.

Now the spaceship started its way to the second drop location in San Francisco.

The confused scouts found themselves standing on that grassy area. In front of them stood a large and strange monument that somehow reminded them of their home planet. Unknown to them, they were standing on the grassy area of the "Watts Towers" monument, located in the heart of Los Angeles' Watts neighborhood.

Meanwhile, the spaceship was on its way north on its second leg of the journey toward the city of San Francisco. The pilot desired to take the longer, slower route via the Pacific Coast Highway with its beautiful scenery. It was something he had picked up from the images on the California's postcards back home, but the rest of the scouts on board contested. They were too tired and didn't care for any scenery or long, winding roads. Complaining they had motion sickness, they insisted on taking the shorter way to their destination. The pilot was irritated with the whining scouts, but was too tired to fight and decided not to argue. He gave up to the pressure and diverted the spaceship to the shorter and boring road, California Highway 5. Three minutes later the spaceship was hovering above the "City by the Bay".

In all fairness, they could have passed that same distance in only two minutes, but the pilot who was still frustrated with his passengers and the forced route change, used that additional minute to look for any attractive scenery on that boring Highway.

Needless to say, nothing is attractive on California Highway 5, not today and not during the Sixties.

Hovering above the city of San Francisco, the spaceship encountered even worse parking issues and, once again, had to maneuver for two days across the city's skies.

Those parking delays were a new thing to worry about and a revelation to the pilot. It made him wonder how the aliens find parking for their enormous transportation spaceships at the time of the invasion when he had to spend so much time to park his small spacecraft. If he had so many problems transporting two small scouting teams, how complicated would it be for the aliens to transport a whole army? The pilot entered his concerns into the spaceship's logs as an urgent recommendation. He marked it in bold red letters with a double underline, simply stating not to use the large transportation spaceships at the time of the invasion, unless the aliens were planning to purchase a large amount of designated parking spaces in advance.

Although San Francisco's parking situation was much worse than in Los Angeles, it was a beautiful city and the scouts didn't mind hovering above it for the next two days. They actually left the pilot to deal with it while they sat with their faces glued to the spaceship's windows, enjoying the scenery down below.

For the next two days, the pilot performed extreme maneuvers, moving erratically above the city's skies, left and right, up and down in an attempt to land. Finally, he converged on an available parking spot and for the second time, landed the spaceship on Earth's surface. Only then the pilot opened the spaceship's hatch and let the second scout team out. This time, there were no flashing lights or sharp commanding loud voices but the complete opposite. There was no pressure and it seemed that the atmosphere around the spaceship was subdued. That allowed the pilot to take his time and wish the scouts the best of luck, before sealing the spaceship's hatch.

This time the spaceship didn't take off. That parking space became the spot where the pilot shutdown the spaceship's engines and parked it for the duration of the scouting mission, for six months with an optional extension of an additional six months. Even though it didn't seem to be quite the perfect parking spot, it was the only one the pilot could find and he didn't want to risk losing it. But in 1967, unknowingly to him, it happened to be the perfect parking spot as it was on one of San Francisco's most famous intersections, exactly at the crossing of two streets, two very specific streets in a very specific location.

Yes, that specific intersection was special and famous as it was located in a place that during the sixties accepted anything and everything that was weird and unusual and if you don't know - an alien spaceship is an ideal fit to this category. Without his knowledge, the pilot landed and parked the spaceship on the corner of Haight and Ashbury streets, in the heart of the same famous neighborhood that carried those streets' names and as it turned out, in 1967 no one in the Haight Ashbury district seemed to care.

Meanwhile, while all of this transpired in Northern California, the Los Angeles scout team had regained their composure and started assessing their immediate environment. They were right smack in the middle of the famous Watts neighborhood, located in the south eastern part of Los Angeles. What made this neighborhood so famous was a chain of events that had transpired two years prior to their arrival. In 1965, this neighborhood was in the center of the famous "Watts Riots" that changed this neighborhood's residents forever. That in itself was something that turned the scouts' mission into an extraordinary one as it was about to change them as well.

You see, during the sixties the Watts's population was predominantly black, poor working class. After years of social injustice, in 1965, this neighborhood exploded with violent riots in an attempt to confront the authorities' discrimination against its residents. Their demands were nothing short of social equality and they were willing to use almost any means possible to achieve justice.

The residents only craved to improve their lives, so they could live in dignity in what they considered to be the "White Man's World." In 1965 it considered as an almost impossible task and as tensions grew, the riots exploded, turning the neighborhood into a war zone. The residents were in need of support and were willing to accept any outsider who aligned himself with their struggle. They went as far as joining forces with the more radical Black Panther movement, which was established a year earlier.

The Black Panthers preached the doctrine of fighting police brutality against black neighborhoods with violence, and encouraged the neighborhood residents to adopt their anti-government views, hoping that their collective voices would resonate throughout the rest of the country.

That helped in influencing the residents' views of the government and state officials. They were voicing, out loud, their anti-government views and plastered the neighborhood walls with radical posters with slogans like "Power to the People" and "Black Power." The residents who viewed the police with suspicion didn't welcome them in the neighborhood and demonstrations against local authorities were a daily occurrence. They were contrived from a mix of the local residents and the Black Panther members who were dressed with their unmistakable attire, which was composed of a white T-shirt covered by a black leather jacket, dark shades and black beret. They would raise their right fist in the air and shout slogans while confronting the local Police. Well, it just happened that in 1967 the alien scouts were dropped by their pilot right in the middle of this explosive situation.

Yes, by now the scouts left the grassy area behind and entered the neighborhood's streets. Still confused from their rude awakening, they were trying to get their bearings. Since it was their first encounter with the humans, they were inching forward cautiously not sure what to expect. To their surprise they were welcomed by the local residents. You see, when the neighborhood residents who were normally suspicious of any outsiders laid their eyes, for the first time, on the purple scouts they accepted them with open arms. As it happened, for one reason or another, the residents believed the scouts to be another discriminated group.

You must understand that during the sixties, the unfortunate fact was that those residents were judged by the color of their skin and not for who they were. When they encountered the dark purple aliens, they were fast to associate them as one more minority group. The hidden truth was that those purple-looking aliens somewhat elevated the local residents feelings. For the first time it dawned on them that there was another minority group out there, which seemed to be way below themselves on the food chain. In secret, those residents who always felt as second-class citizens, were happy to welcome the aliens, believing them to be a third-class citizens. Assuming the aliens were mistreated by the same government who mistreated them, the Watts residents made it a priority to nurture the aliens, who for them seemed to be lost, confused and out of place.

They took the aliens under their wings and started educating them with their life views, the point of view of the black society of 1967. As for the scouts, they gladly accepted the residents' input, as one of their objectives was to adapt and study their immediate environment, the human way of life. A short time after, the scouts were able to conclude that demonstrations were a normal part of the human society, a natural part of their behavior. Considering it all, that wasn't the case with the Watts residents during the sixties. In their situation, they had every right to demonstrate this social injustice, they had a very good reason. But in today's world we have grown to believe that it is good to demonstrate against anything and everything and since we consider demonstration as a synonym to complaint – today we are very good at "demonstrating".

It wasn't long before the scouts found themselves participating in the residents' daily activities, which mostly revolved around anti-government and anti-war demonstrations. At the end of the day, when the sun set and everyone were winding down, they would join the residents in their gatherings, which lasted until the early hours of the morning, to discuss the day's events. Slowly, those activities became the scouts' new reality. A short time later they were able to develop their own opinions about the "White Men, Black Men, Purple Alien" relationships.

As time passed, they found themselves more and more attached to their new friends and truly started to assimilate into their environment, which was reflected in their newly found anti-government views and adoption of the black culture and jive slang. Above all it was the Black Panthers' fashion that influenced the aliens. The Los Angeles scouts started wearing the Panthers' signature attire and every so often raised their right arm with its clutched claws for no apparent reason.

In comparison to them, it was a cakewalk for their counterparts in San Francisco. They emerged from the parked spaceship right into the middle of the Haight and Ashbury intersection. Standing in the middle of any other cross streets of the city would be a death wish, but that wasn't the case in 1967 in terms of these two cross streets. The scouts immediately realized that by any account they were in a very special place, which allowed them to merge with the local human society with no problems.

And they were correct. In 1967 there was no other neighborhood as famous as the Haight Ashbury district of San Francisco. After all, it was the time of cultural changes and Haight Ashbury had become the ground zero, the Mecca if you would, of the Hippies and the counterculture movement. The Hippie movement was interesting but also important to our country's history as it introduced to us and the rest of the world new cultural changes. It was reflected in music, free spirit, free love, experimental drugs, and most important, in very poor personal hygiene choices.

Most of all, the Hippies were peace loving and believed in sharing, living harmoniously with nature and, obviously, in the end of the Vietnam War. They were also on a collision course with the authorities, demonstrating daily to end the overseas conflict that claimed so many young lives. As the Watts residents, the Hippies were willing to accept help from any outsider.

But unlike the Los Angeles residents, when the alien spaceship maneuvered for two days above the city of San Francisco, the majority of Haight Ashbury residents were not alarmed. You see, most of them were under the influence of one psychedelic drug or another, so their reaction was somewhat different than expected in a situation like that. Amazingly, or maybe expectedly, unlike the Los Angeles residents, the Hippies didn't rush to the nearest phone booth to report the strange phenomenon above them. Instead, they gathered on rooftops, in small groups, and enjoyed the bright light show above them, which was composed from erratically moving lights, up and down, left and right. They lit a fresh joint and passed it around while admiring that free happening in the skies, giggling and mumbling to one another: **"Wow man, look at those lights. Look at those colors, this is so FAR OUT."**

Simply saying, the Hippies were too stoned to link those erratic lights with UFO sightings, but I'm certain that they did appreciate that once in a lifetime colorful cosmic event.

And if I'm certain of one more thing is that in 1967 "Lady Luck" shone on the San Francisco scouts. Actually, that same lady shined on anyone who was in the notorious Haight Ashbury district in the summer of 1967 as they were very lucky as well. Ask any of the 100,000 hippies, from all over the world, who were at that specific time period in this neighborhood and they will tell you that it was one of the most memorable moments in the Hippie movement and the history of world music.

It just happened that the summer of 1967 was the exact time of the famous and memorable "Summer of Love" festival.

My guess is that some of you, especially the young ones among you, are wondering what the "Summer of Love" festival was all about and what made it so special and memorable?

Well, let me tell you. During the sixties, San Francisco was able to establish itself as the county's most important gathering place for the counterculture movement. It actually became its front line in the fight for social and political changes. And if San Francisco was the center, Haight Ashbury district was the epicenter. This small district's streets were crowded with young people who believed in the freedom of speech, life and expression. There was no better place in both infrastructure and atmosphere for a festival like the "Summer of Love" festival to spring up.

Imagine an enormous amount of Hippies from every corner of the world, converging on that very small district, demanding the end of the Vietnam War and protesting social injustice. They were on a quest for freedom through political changes and was there any better way to accomplish their task other than in one great music festival?

It was a huge celebration, one big Hippie party. Now, have you ever heard of any good party that didn't have good music? Well, this party wasn't any different. It didn't just have good music but great music by some of the greatest bands of all times like: the Jefferson Airplane, the Grateful Dead and the icing on the cake - "The Jimi Hendrix Experience."

Yes, Jimi was there performing in the 1967 "Summer of Love" festival!

But it was much more than just a great music festival and one of its most important outcomes was the formal recognition of the Hippies and the counterculture movement. It was the first time for the country to understand that movement's influence in promoting social changes. The Hippies were able to change people's views, opening our eyes to recognize social injustice against certain segments of our society, allowing us to better grasp the power of one. We were capable of innovating, to change the existing status quo and improve our lives in the process. The Hippies' communal life reminded us that we were not alone in the fight.

It wasn't hard for the scouts to recognize their good fortune and they bluntly used it to their advantage. It reflected in their first action, which wasn't exactly on their objectives list. Unlike the Los Angeles scouts, they didn't attempt to initiate first contact with the local population or start the search for the highly coveted replacement "Double AA" batteries. What they did was to contact their counterparts in Los Angeles and, show off their good fortune.

Right after, they rushed up the street to the Golden Gate Park, where Jimi Hendrix had a live performance. It was an energizing concert that ended in the late hours of the night, leaving the scouts with no other logical alternative, but to continue partying until the early morning hours. By then, they were pretty jazzed up and had to spend the rest of the day winding down. Only then they started focusing on their mission's first objective, interacting with the local population, the Hippies. That would be an understatement. The scouts found that objective to be one of the most challenging, yet intriguing part of their mission.

They also approached their target cautiously and guess what? They as well were welcomed by the Hippies with open arms, no questions asked. The Hippies, who at that time were considered the outcasts of our society, accepted the purple creatures they mistakenly assumed to be just another outcast group. Deep inside, like the Watts residents, the Hippies had great relief to know that there was another group out there, which seemed to be in a lower position than them on the outcast chart.

The stoned Hippies confused the purple creatures for another group mistreated by our society. It never crossed their minds that there was a future intergalactic conflict brewing right in front of them on Earth's surface. Anyway, they were too busy to worry about intergalactic conflicts as they were still dealing with a local conflict called "The Vietnam War." They had enough on their plate and the last thing they needed was another headache. As for the aliens' physical appearance, the Hippies thought it was a distortion, a side effect created in their mind, a result of their excessive use of psychedelic drugs.

I'm aware that in today's very logical world, it sounds absurd and illogical reasoning, but during the nostalgic Sixties, at the times of the Hippies' drug induced era, this statement made a lot of sense.

Needless to say that from the scouts' point of view, their first encounter with the Hippies, made them suspect that there was something slightly off with those humans – not wrong but off. At times it seems as the Hippies were just spacing out in the middle of any conversation, no matter the topic. All you had to do was try to engage them in conversation and out of nowhere they would start admiring the imaginary flowers on your shirt and the glow around you. Sometimes, when the scouts approached them in an attempt to gain a grasp of the new language, the Hippies would just stare back with a blank look and say something like: **"Hey Man, you are looking kind of funny... WOW, look at those beautiful flowers."** That would make the scouts leave the conversation with nothing gained and nothing lost.

Maybe the Hippies were weird and awkward, but still they played a major role in the changes that took over the San Francisco scouts. The more time the scouts spent with them the faster their transformation took place. The Hippies introduced them to a new world, made out of sharing, happiness, love, and peace. In the Hippies laid-back world, there were no worries about tomorrow and the scouts couldn't find a reason to shield themselves from such concept. They were sucked into that same world and in return lost their edge. They fell in love with this alternative way of life. It was a colorful world populated by a group of social misfits who found a common ground that was drizzled with flowers and a very colorful choice of clothing.

Yes, the San Francisco scouts were no different from their Los Angeles counterparts. They also fell in love with their immediate environment's fashion, the Hippies' fashion. Just as the Black Panthers fashion, the Hippies' fashion carried a powerful statement. But contrary to the Black Panthers' harsh message with their stark, black and white apparel, the Hippies communicated to the aliens that there was an alternative way to achieve your goals without resorting to violence, indicative of their colorful Tie-dyed and flowery garb. Observing the Hippies, the scouts learned another important piece of information about humans' communication skills. As the scouts saw it, to achieve good communication – it is a must to have flowers on hand.

And it wasn't far from the true. In the sixties, Hippies and flowers were synonymous and you can say that they went hand in hand, a fact that not just went unnoticed by the scouts, but was embraced by them as a necessity during human interaction. Later, the San Francisco scouts would strongly recommend implementing this conduct at the time of the invasion. They marked it as an entry in their report, stating that any future human contact must start with a gesture of flowers handout, preferably daisies. In their perception, flowers had a direct link to the human heart and a way to lower its guard. Using the Hippies doctrine, at face value, they believed that this gesture would allow them to invade our planet while avoiding the use of force.

The scouts admired the Hippies' laid-back lifestyle and found themselves drawn to it. As they got closer to the Hippies, they also started experimenting with their hallucinogenic drugs, and from that point on there was nothing to stop them from taking an active role in the Hippies' gatherings, which were mainly composed of demonstrations and all-night parties. You could easily spot them in the front lines of the Hippies' peace rallies, and I am sure that a closer inspection of the 1967 Hippies' protests photos would expose some purple entities holding anti-war signs. Well, they were also very easy to spot in the feminist movement's protests, standing among the protestors, singing and chanting, unknowingly involving themselves in the fight for women's equality. I guess that it could be attributed to the magic of the language barrier.

At night they would crash with their Hippie buddies in one of the communal houses or grassy fields on the outskirts of San Francisco. They would lie down on their backs, sharing a joint with the Hippies while gazing at the endless skies above. They were drifting with their thoughts, maybe even thinking about the small purple planet they had left behind.

Decades later, long after the Vietnam War, we returned to our boring lives and began to reflect on our society's failures during the sixties. Only then did we realize how we had mistreated our own, the ones who fought for our country, which in return didn't fight for them. But since we are humans, we didn't reflect for long. As always, we let our ideology take a back seat and put greed right back in front of it. By then, most Hippies had cut their hair short, shaved their beards, stashed away their tie-dyed clothing and became lawyers and CPAs. They became very serious people who owned houses with a pool and a two car garage, married to a loving wife and had a kid or two. In some cases they even owned a dog and a membership at the neighborhood health club.

Those ex-Hippies or "Yuppies", as they were called, knew better so they taught their kids to stay away from drugs, premarital sex and loud music. They also taught them of the importance of education, the value of a sharp looking front lawn and the advantage of a new car in the driveway; you know, the more important things in life.

They made sure not to speak about their younger years and their drug-induced experiences. Only on rare occasions, when their children were already asleep and friends came over for dinner, only then it would happen. They would sit in their living room, enjoying one more glass of wine when the conversation about the magical sixties would arise. They would mention that crazy time period and reminisce on their experiences. Then on the edge of their consciousness, they would find themselves clinging to fuzzy memories of short, purple, funny looking creatures that somehow were linked to their past Hippie lives.

They would remember aliens wearing tie-dyed T-shirts, chanting in gibberish, holding a joint in their claws. They would mention a weird re-occurring dream that visits them every so often, something about "Time Capsules," a damaged spaceship's left side, and replacement "Double AA" batteries.

Talking with their eyes closed, opening their hearts in their living rooms, they would do their monologue. They would open their eyes only to see the shock on their friends' faces and the horror in their wives' eyes, believing that their husbands had just lost it. That would be the cue for them to dismiss it all and attribute those visions to their past Hippie lifestyle – highly over-inflated, of course, and switch the conversation to junior's last baseball practice.

But as the evening ended, they would escort their guests to their cars, telling their wives to go inside ahead of them as they needed to check the mailbox. They would take the mail and walk back toward the house only to stop in their tracks and for no apparent reason, gaze at the starry skies. They would stand there, looking at the universe above, allowing a single thought to cross their minds. Just standing there, they would wonder what exactly they were looking for in those starry skies.

During the sixties there was a new notion that everything was possible. The San Francisco scouts made sure to exploit this notion down to a tee, getting involved with every aspect of the Hippies' lifestyle, making sure to party as hard as they could. During the "Summer of Love" festival, they took advantage of this once in a lifetime opportunity to jump on the event main stage and perform with the encouragement of the cheering Hippie crowd. It happened during the short break between "The Who" and "The Grateful Dead" appearances. The stage was deserted for a few moments and the scouts didn't have a second thought. They jumped on it, picked up some of the instruments that were left behind and started playing and singing their top five alien songs. To allow the humans to make some sense of their melody, they had to play and sing backwards. Let's just say that it sounded less like their ordinary alien beat and more like Yoko Ono in her younger days. Nevertheless, the stoned Hippies didn't notice the difference and wildly cheered the aliens who felt as if they had just scored big with the humans. It was a perfect night for them, but they were completely unaware that they were about to score even bigger.

You see, at the end of their "gig", the scouts were rushed or, more accurately, escorted by security backstage were everything was hectic. They were confused from all the commotion and the stage employees that were running at all directions, but suddenly nothing matter anymore. Everything just stopped around them and they felt as they were walking on clouds. They had a glimpse of Jimi Hendrix who was backstage, sitting all alone in one corner, the man and his guitar. They could recognize him from the tour brochures, his unmistakable hairdo and the bright violet bandana that held it up high. Without missing a beat, they lost the security personnel and walked directly to him.

It would be the first time for the aliens to meet Jimi, in person. They wasted no time on introductions and engaged him in conversation. Being that excited, they bombarded him with questions, mainly about his music.

Jimi, on his part, was cool as a can be and felt comfortable around what he considered to be short purple aliens. More surprisingly, he had no problem carrying conversation with them even though he didn't know their language. He spoke English while the aliens replied in their native tongue and yet they were able to understand each other. This wouldn't happened with any other human on Earth, not during the scouting mission and not during the invasion itself, but it happened with Jimi Hendrix.

The aliens were not surprised, to them Jimi was more than just another human – he was a divine entity. Is there any other way to explain his divine music?

The aliens knew they were on borrowed time and wanted to use it wisely so they made sure not to mention the "Time Capsule," their damaged spaceship, the Tape Player or the search for the replacement "Double AA" batteries. Initially they handled Jimi as a supreme being, kind enough to give them some of his time, but soon after they found him to be a really "down to Earth" kind of guy, a cool cat. It made them even bolder and they moved from asking questions to submitting requests. They actually asked him to teach them the art of mastering a guitar, but shortly after realized that since they had claws for fingers, it was an impossible task. Teaching them how to play with their teeth was completely out of the question as their teeth were too sharp and would clearly damage the guitar strings. In return for his kindness, the aliens teach Jimi how to hide secret messages in his tunes, messages that could only be understood by the aliens.

Those are the kind of messages one can hear only if you played the tune at a faster speed. Play the vinyl record at regular speed for the humans to enjoy but increase the speed of your player and the vinyl will decode a message in the aliens' language. Jimi was grateful and promised to use this new found knowledge. There are rumors that he actually implemented it in one of his tunes "Third Stone from the Sun." You should try it. Play this tune at the regular speed and you can hear a story about the alien scouts. Increase the playing speed and you will hear Jimi's hidden message to his alien friends.

I just remembered that vinyl records are not that available today but I have a 21st-century solution. Google it!!! It is fascinating.

No one knows for sure what this message is all about, but most likely it is something like this:

"Hey You Cool Cats, It was rocking to meet you. I loved the conversation. Why don't you keep a spare seat on your next visit, just in case...

See you in 1970, Peace & Love, JIMI."

The scouts spent the next six months among us humans. The Los Angeles team merged with the radical and somewhat agitated Black Panthers while the San Francisco team communed with the laid back Hippies.

After six months, both scout teams found an excuse to initiate the optional six months extension. It seems as they were having too much fun on Earth and didn't want to return to their planet. In contrast, the scouts justified their request, blaming it on the nature of the complicated human society. There was no other way to really study us without using those additional six months, they declared. To prove their point they reminded their supervisor of that ongoing barrage of rockets, the humans were still shooting, for no apparent reason, toward that small innocent and most important <u>vacant</u> rock that spun aimlessly around their plant. Since none of the aliens had a logic explanation for that mystery, the scouts were granted the additional six months stay.

In their favor, it is fair to say that while they were enjoying their time among us, they also did their best to collect information about us, to investigate our every move in preparation for the future invasion. But if you take into consideration the Black Panther and the Hippie movements' social standing in 1967, you can understand how that information, collected by the scouts, didn't represent the true nature of our society as a whole. Actually, it was pretty much incorrect and misleading. Since those two groups held completely different and polarized views from each other, the scouts' intelligence work couldn't do more than give the aliens' high command a headache and all the wrong ideas about us.

Completely oblivious to that, the two teams continued taking their notes and assembling their respective reports while making sure to keep involved with their human friends' daily events. The Los Angeles scouts always found time to protest the white man's oppression of the black man. At the same time, the San Francisco scouts were always available for a trip to the fields outside the city to collect fresh flowers and share them amongst the protesting but surprisingly happy Hippies.

Above all, both teams never missed the chance to visit Jimi in his live performances. They followed his scheduled appearances across the west coast, and were easy to trace no matter how large the crowd. This was not surprising since they were the noisiest fans of all, chanting his songs out loud in their alien tongue.

As you can see, the scouts' first objective was fairly easy to accomplish. They were very successful in integrating with their immediate environment. Their acceptance, with no questions asked, by both the Black Panthers and Hippies made this objective even easier to complete.

It was the second objective, the urgent one, which proved itself harder to fulfill and frustrating for both teams. The search for the replacement batteries turned into an unsuccessful endeavor. Those little elusive devices that were so crucial for the sanity of their entire alien nation became a major obstacle in their mission's success.

The scouts made every effort to put their claws on those mysterious devices. They even made sure that the first sentence they learned in the humans' language was: *"Need Batteries, Good Price."*

Since they had no proven way to acquire those rare items, they developed their own method. Hiding in dark alleys, between buildings, the scouts waited for passing humans and whispered, with a strongly accented, scratchy voice, that same sentence while stretching their long arm forward and exposing one of the expired batteries they had brought with them.

Now, as we all know humans do not respond that well to anyone that just pop out from dark alleys and mumbling something in a thick foreign accent while stretching his arm forward and exposing suspicious items, especially if that someone is dark short and purple looking. Those kind of encounters will always result with a rattled human who believes that his life is in danger and leaves the scene at double speed and a new tale under his belt for his friends and family.

This method was an utter failure, and since it didn't enable them to obtain even a single battery, the scouts left with no other choice but to fall back on extreme measures, their last option. They will approach their adopting human groups for help. After all, nowhere in their list of objectives was it stated that they couldn't mix the two objectives. Why couldn't they use the same society they were scouting to find those replacement batteries for them? Could there be any reason for the humans to refuse their request?

They went forward with their plans and not only did it fail to produce positive results, but started a firestorm within the two groups. The Los Angeles scouts approached their Black Panther friends only to be scolded by them. Apparently, the Black Panthers got very upset, telling the scouts that besides being poor and they wouldn't put one red cent in the white man's pocket, they didn't use expensive batteries anyhow, but rather inexpensive candles. The Black Panthers made sure to finish their scolding by providing the scouts with some candles. They also asked them never to raise this subject again.

Unlike the Black Panthers, the Haight Ashbury district Hippies had no financial issues. Still, they almost had a fit when the San Francisco scouts approached them with the same request. The Hippies immediately organized a three-hour sit-down with the scouts. It was a long lecture, more like an intervention, about the dark side of those devices called "Batteries." The Hippies, who were environmentally conscious at heart, told the scouts about the pollution produced by these devil-made creations and emphasized the urgency in keeping our planet clean and green.

They finished their lecture, requesting the scouts never to mention this crazy idea again and to show the scouts that they were not upset with them, the Hippies handed the scouts their alternative solution for batteries.

Yes, it was the same kind of inexpensive candles, and yes, there were flowers attached to them, and yes, those flowers were arranged in the shape of a peace sign. Only then the Hippies left the scouts alone with their thoughts, shaken and exhausted.

Their last attempt left them frustrated and with no other choice, but to add one more conclusion to their reports. Both teams concluded that replacement "Double AA" batteries were a thing of the past, impossible to get, and most likely a figment of the imagination.

It is true that the scouts have changed. They were not the same, not in their exterior and not in their mind set. They were able to assimilate to their immediate environment and even act as the humans in their close proximity, but there is one thing I must tell you.

It might be a small detail, but those scouts acted as the delicate connection between the Black Panther and Hippie movements in 1967.

Although both groups were in a fight for the same causes, to end social injustice and discrimination while pursuing social changes, they were miles apart in the differences of their methods. Each group also held its own idea about the Vietnam War. The Hippies, who were mainly composed of a young, white majority, wanted to end the war, while the Black Panthers, who obviously originated from a young black minority, protested the drafting of young black men, against their will, to fight the "White Man's" war. The members of the two movements came from different backgrounds and life experiences.

Other than the fact that they were using the same kind of inexpensive candles they were completely polarized and disconnected, but it was a given that they needed each other's help. Up to that point the groups' lack of connection was unbridgeable. And then came along our short purple aliens.

To my knowledge, those two movements' first interaction was a direct result of that crucial communication the San Francisco scouts initiated with their Los Angeles counterparts, right after their arrival in the middle of the "Summer of Love" festival and their encounter with Jimi Hendrix. Overcome with jealousy, the Los Angeles scouts presented the Black Panther members Jimi's tour brochure and begged them to take them as soon as they could to that magical place called the "Haight Ashbury District."

The Black Panthers weren't that keen to spend six hours with the purple creatures in the same vehicle, but couldn't figure another way to shut them up. So, they gave in to the scout's nagging and they all climbed into an orange and white Volkswagen mini-bus and started the long, sorry road trip to San Francisco. The truth was that while the scouts sought to reach San Francisco just in time for Jimi's next show their drivers, the Black Panthers, had their own agenda for this excursion. They were curious about Jimi Hendrix, the great black artist that aligned himself between the two movements. They had a need in his support, knowing that the magnitude of his star power and influence could only help their fight. Secretly, they were even hoping to recruit Jimi to their cause.

A short time into the drive, still within the Los Angeles city limits, it dawned on the Black Panthers that a six-hour road trip could feel like a lifetime when your passengers are funny-looking, purple creatures, speaking what sounded like gibberish. The excited scouts couldn't keep quiet, or stop asking in their native tongue, "Are we there yet? Are we there yet? Are we there yet?" It didn't stop until the mini-van reached San Francisco's suburbs.

In the Sixties the members of the Black Panther movement swore to keep some strict commitments. Among them were their commitments to their race, their community, and their party's cause. They swore to guard those commitments with their lives, but after this crucial road trip they made sure to add one additional new commitment to their charter. They pledged to never, ever,

ever, ever take excited short purple creatures on a road trip lasting longer than five minutes, round trip. Ever!!

Finally, the VW mini-bus reached the city center, passed through its famous attractions and drove straight to the Haight Ashbury district. It barely reached a full stop when the eager scouts jumped out at the sight of their waiting friends. They rushed to them and were welcomed with their newly learned slang, **"Hey brothers, what's shaking? So this are the new cats, you told us about? Power to the People, man – Can you dig it?"**

Restless and excited the Los Angeles scouts ignored the small talk and bombarded their friends with questions: **Where is he? How was his show? Are we on time for the next show? Why are you looking at me like that? What do you mean - what a beautiful flowers?? HEY, stop staring at us like that!!**

The San Francisco scouts didn't say a word. Instead, they grabbed the Los Angeles scouts by their arms and took them and their Black Panther friends back to the Golden Gate Park, backstage to Jimi's dressing room, where they were introduced to Jimi. Needless to say, it was an unforgettable moment for the Los Angeles scouts who, obviously, felt though everything stopped around them and they were walking on clouds. Not wasting any more time they started asking Jimi the exact same questions that the San Francisco scouts had. The Black Panther members were no different; they used this golden opportunity to lecture Jimi about their cause, openly asking for his support, insisting that his fame could only help his black brothers in their ongoing crusade for social fairness.

It was an intense conversation in which the Black Panthers realized there were some gaps they had to bridge. Eavesdropping on the conversation, you could hear free-spirited Jimi Hendrix saying out loud:

"But I am a Hippie!!!" and the Black Panthers responding with: *"Yes you are! No question about it but you are also..."* waiting for Jimi to finish the sentence.

Jimi delayed his response, trying to understand what the Black Panthers were trying to convey to him. It wasn't that Jimi had forgotten his origins or the color of his skin, but much simpler than that. It was a Jimi Hendrix original. You see, Jimi never considered his race an obstacle in his development as person or artist. He never felt limited in his quest for creativity and when this fact was raised by the Black Panthers, he was confused by it.

Nevertheless, he assured them of his support in their cause and even gave them the permission to adopt his song "Voodoo Child" as their anthem, which I believe they did.

If you really think about it, Jimi Hendrix was different. He was special; the only entity that could bridge the gap between the Hippies and the Black Panthers, the only one who could engage with both groups and act as a medium. After all, he was the most famous black, free-spirited person of the Sixties.

If there is a fact that shouldn't go unnoticed is that Jimi Hendrix was the only artist who was loved not just by the two movements who oppose the Vietnam War, but also by the young servicemen who were fighting it overseas.

Funny enough, out of all the living, breathing life forms on Earth in 1967, our purple alien scouts were the only ones who took notice of it.

Now, the scouts were able to connect the dots and have a better understanding of their mystical attraction to Jimi and his music. Jimi wasn't just another human being, but a higher entity capable to perform magical wonders with his music and electric guitar, a treasure that from one strange reason had chosen planet Earth as his home. If you consider the winds of times you'll see that through his music and lyrics, Jimi Hendrix did perform miracles. He played for everyone, ignored everything and did anything just the way he wanted to. Ultimately, Jimi was able to achieve what he craved to do most - to entertain everyone even if it meant moving through time and place. He did so with great success, reaching everyone, everywhere, his countryman both in the USA and overseas and even a whole alien colony on a faraway galaxy.

As we all know, Jimi Hendrix succeeded in creating timeless music that encapsulated his unique personality, bound for eternity with his timeless image. The scouts knew this as well. They concluded that their journey across galaxies to obtain replacement batteries with the sole purpose to allow them to maintain the hold on his music was justified. They added this very important conclusion to their reports.

The scouts spent the next two days in Jimi's company. The Black Panther members who were in desperate need for some quiet time, excused themselves and drove across the bridge to Oakland, the birth city of their movement, to visit their party headquarters. For them, it was a much needed rest and at the end of the second day they, reluctantly, returned to collect the scouts on their way back to Los Angeles. This time, they've made sure to equip themselves with earplugs, they purchased in advance from a small local drug store. After all, experience does count.

The additional six months flew by, and the scouts' mission was coming to its end. There were no more excuses and since the scouts had become accustomed to the humans' way of life, they couldn't bear the thought of leaving it all behind.

You must understand that after spending a whole year among us, they had everything but a house mortgage and a car lease. In the course of that year, they managed to build a small, private corner for themselves, something they called home. It was a place to live and relax, far from the humans' fast and crazy-paced life on Earth. It had a doorbell and pictures on the walls. That place belonged to them even though it was a rental.

They had no desire to leave it all behind, but found comfort in the knowledge they would return at the time of the invasion. While packing their equipment and finalizing their affairs, they also made sure to extend their rental agreements for five years, all paid in advance, and secure the low monthly rent. They made a visit to the post office and signed all the necessary paperwork to ensure that their mail would be held for the next three years. Only then they were the able to concentrate on finalizing their mission reports, summarizing their collected information about their Earthly encounters and conclusions.

Not surprisingly, both reports had the same conclusion of the highly desired and still unobtainable replacement "Double AA" batteries. In the scouting teams' eyes those batteries were one big mystery, apparently impossible to acquire and, most likely, didn't exist. The scouts suggested a full-scale invasion with a large amount of alien soldiers, all equipped with at least two set of eyes to cover as much ground as they could in the pursuit for the replacement batteries. They emphasized that the more aliens meant the more sets of fresh eyes. As you can see, they had spent plenty time with us to learn how to avoid taking responsibility for their shortcomings. In their eyes, reporting that "Made in California, USA, Double AA batteries" didn't exist in California, USA was better than admitting a failure.

The last task on their list was to pack their personal belongings and then came what the scouts later described as the hardest part of their mission – the return home. I'm not definite if the difficult part was their leaving of Earth or the return to their purple planet and their old way of life. Their collective colorful experiences on our planet had left a deep impression on their souls, making it unthinkable for them to return to what they considered a boring purple planet. They didn't want to abandon the new life they became accustomed to. For them, returning home was like returning from a great vacation they wished would never end. I'm sure it sounds familiar and at one time or another you felt the same.

No wonder they wanted to stay on Earth. You see, of all places they could touchdown, they had been lucky enough to spend a whole year in sunny California. As they were getting ready for their return, they felt depleted and didn't want to assist the pilot with the spaceship's preparations before the long flight. It was parked for a whole year at the same place, on the corner of Haight and Ashbury, and in need of some attention. They had no intention of dealing with the enormous electric bill accumulated during the spaceship's power plant recharging. I can't begin to describe how impatient they were while standing in line in the crowded San Francisco City Hall to pay the hundreds of parking citations, left throughout the year on the spaceship's windshield.

They wanted to stay on Earth. They felt depressed, but if there was one thing that somewhat cheered them, it was the hiring of a detailing company, which removed the spider webs and dust from the parking spaceship and brought it back to "spick and span" condition. Oh yes, considering everything they went through, including their current state of mind, the scouts never forgot to fly in style.

What made it so hard for them to leave? Well, it was the same small and insignificant things we, humans, take for granted. It was the late afternoon sunsets over the Pacific Ocean, the bonfire gatherings with the background music and friendly conversations, it was the California mellow way of life. In a bizarre way, it was also about the humans they met and were leaving behind, the residents of the two neighborhoods who had accepted them with open arms. The scouts learned how to appreciate the intense Black Panthers and the easy going Hippies, for good reason. You see, even with their metallic eyes they were able to see that behind the rough and tough Black Panthers or the laid back Hippies, behind their behavior and the garments, they were human, after all.

It's funny to hear such deep thought coming from a purple alien, but you must agree that sometimes the best point of view is the one we've never heard before. After all, there is nothing better than a new perspective from an outsider, a remote uncle you see only during the holidays or a purple alien from a faraway galaxy.

If there was one more thing the scouts dearly cared about, it was their interaction with Jimi Hendrix and the friendship that had sparked between them during their long stay on Earth. While on Earth, they were following Jimi up and down the California coastline, always making sure to have the time for long and meaningful conversations backstage. Before their departure, they visited Jimi for the last time, but this time there was no time for conversation. Instead, without many words, the scouts handed Jimi a gift, their most important prized possession. It was the two "Double AA" drained batteries they had brought with them from their home planet. They didn't see a reason to carry those batteries back home and since they gave Jimi the highest respect, they believed that he deserved to own such precious items.

Jimi, for his part, wasn't sure what it was all about, but after spending one long year with the quirky scouts, assumed there must be a good reason for this unusual gift. He took the batteries and right there made a promise. He told them he would keep those batteries with him at all times.

Only then the scouts felt like they were ready for the flight home. After settling the parking citations and upon a vigorous inspection of the spaceship's detailing job, the two teams were ready to board the spaceship and leave Earth.

The scouts' departure from Earth's surface was also entered into the aliens' historical records. The formal chain of events was described in a very short paragraph. It all started with the pilot and the San Francisco scouts lifting off from the parking spot in Haight Ashbury on their way south, en route to Los Angeles. This time the passengers kept quiet when the pilot chose to take the longer and beautiful Pacific Coast Highway to Los Angeles. The spaceship reached the grassy area in front of the Watts Towers monument and the waiting Los Angeles scouts. They quickly boarded the spaceship and, after a second and final head count, the spaceship began its long trip home. Well, that was at least the official version…

Chapter 4 – The Scouts Return

It would be an understatement to say that the returning scouts were changed aliens from the ones who had landed on Earth a year earlier. Their time on Earth had definitely changed them, and now on board the returning spaceship something else was revealed. The two teams had become completely different from one another. Their unique experiences had enhanced their individuality and altered their perspectives on life. They came to Earth as one united group and left as two polarized groups, with different opinions about life, the human race, Earth and even the upcoming invasion, not to mention their opposite opinions about fashion. With this new reality, the two groups were sitting facing each other, in two lines, in the confined space of the small, crowded spaceship.

It might be hard for us to understand the magnitude of our earthly ways and the effect it could have on innocent extraterrestrial beings. Whether it was only a passing by alien or one who wants to get acquainted with a primitive life form, or maybe just an alien on a scouting mission, preparing for a future full scale invasion, the impact on their personalities was tremendous.

You see, when your planet is shapeless, blurry, and purple, with no gravitational environment or natural source of light the probability of any radical change of life is close to zero. This is when our planet turn into a very delightful place.

More than that, if you happened to land on our planet and experience our way of life, you would change sooner than you think. Shockingly, it is very easy for any alien to get hooked on even the smallest things we offer such as "Double AA" batteries – not that we ever offer anything for free.

When we Count our lifetime achievements we become cynical. We believe our achievements couldn't contribute much to what we consider an advanced life form. How can we humans influence advanced life forms? Especially, if you take into account the kind of aliens who possess such technology that allows them to zip across galaxies. Remember, we are talking about the same kind of aliens who are capable of creating gigantic, yet perfect, crop circles in the middle of the night, in total darkness - without a flashlight.

On second thought, we might be overlooking something. Maybe, there is a small chance that humans can contribute to advanced alien societies. Think about it, some of our lifetime creations, even the ones we consider obsolete, might be viewed by aliens as new, advanced and maybe even exciting.

It might happen that an alien who encounters, for the first time, a car wheel or a cigarette lighter would consider them as the most stimulating items he ever came across. By the same token, it might be that his fascination could be influenced by our marketing abilities, which as everyone knows – is pretty amazing. This astounding marketing ability of ours is reflected today in every aspect of our lives. We are so prone to buy into all the nonsense that is marketed to us, weather it is a snake oil medicine, a TV infomercial of weird devices that never work or, unfortunately, all those young untalented singers.

In the sixties it wasn't like that, everything was real, including people. But even then, it seems there was something we, unknowingly marketed to the scouts, which became so appealing to them. It wasn't an item, but a place, a very specific place in a very specific era. It was California of the sixties that was so appealing to the aliens.

As the country was in the midst of the Vietnam War turmoil, California's residents led the way in the quest for freedom and free speech. They believed in their ability to make a change and convince others to follow in their footsteps and it was all done under the umbrella of the Golden State. California was gaining its reputation for its great minds and high-tech innovators who joined hands with the counterculture movement to produce new technological advancements. This state with its mix of cultures was the place that left a strong impression on the visiting scouts and now they were forced to depart. They had to abandon the Hippies and Black Panthers, the music and the love, the all-night political and social gatherings, but they wouldn't go quietly. A later examination of the pilot's sealed flight logs revealed another story of the scouts' departure from the Golden State. That story was very much different from the official one, in their historical records. It seems that some scouts refused to leave California and had to be dragged kicking and screaming into the spaceship.

Furthermore, the log described that even a promise of a poster signed by Jimi Hendrix with a personal dedication didn't do the trick. The only solution was a good whack to the back of their heads that neutralized the stragglers and allowed the pilot to drag them to their chairs.

In any case, the spaceship left Earth's atmosphere and started its voyage home. As the pilot was navigating through our solar system, the mood in the crowded passenger area became tense. The two teams, who were facing each other, started sneering across the aisle. They were from the same planet and the same neighborhood and even had the same upbringing. They came to Earth united on the same mission, but returned home completely polarized. It was even reflected in their views of our political affairs, where each group had its own solution to those affairs.

It seems that the only commonalty they had was their unconditional affection to Jimi Hendrix and even this admiration transpired differently with each team. The Los Angeles team adored his support of the black community and willingness to take a stand in the "White Man's" music scene. Above all, they appreciated his views against the Vietnam War. In comparison to them, the San Francisco team saluted Jimi's association with the free-spirited Hippies. They appreciated how he used his music as a tool to express his spirit and speak his mind. Above all, they appreciated his views against the Vietnam War.

The teams were glaring at each other and a short time after a heated argument erupted across the spaceship's aisle. As the spaceship reached Saturn's Rings, the shouting match escalated and the two teams were an inch away from exchanging blows. It was all the result of a heated argument, were the scouts were expressing their difference of opinions. Curiously, through their actions the scouts almost acted as humans, unable to solve their differences without resulting to physical aggression, the way we handle our arguments. The temper was rising and the situation inside the small spaceship was reaching a boiling point, but that was when the pilot decided to intervene.

To better comprehend the pilot's actions, let me try to describe to you the scene in human terms. Imagine a spaceship at the beginning of a very long journey. It has just left the last gas station with a full tank of gas and some snacks for the road. The pilot made sure his passengers relieved themselves ahead of the long trip as he had no plan to make any stops along the way. Now he was doing his best to navigate through our solar system's surface streets, looking for the galactic highway that would lead him to the moving wormhole and their galaxy. He is already frustrated from the wrong directions given to him by the spaceship's UPS (Universal Positioning System) and only to add fuel to the fire, his backseat passengers started to argue loudly. That made the pilot reach his wits end. In human terms, does this sound familiar?

Still wearing their black berets and leather jackets, the Los Angeles scouts were as radical as their Black Panther friends. They confronted the free-spirited San Francisco scouts, who on their part boarded the departing spaceship wearing colorful tie-died T-shirts and daisy crowns. The last thing on their mind was confrontation and they tried to ease the conflict the best way they knew, or maybe after their long stay on Earth, the only way they knew. They handed the upset Los Angeles scouts fresh flowers, trying to appease them, but this peace offering only made matters worse. The Los Angeles scouts felt patronized by the gesture. Their response was to throw the flowers on the spaceship floor and smash them with their feet.

Their earthly experience had not been as pleasant as their San Francisco counterparts. Feeling discriminated, they carry a chip on their shoulders and considered the flower gesture as one more way of undermining them. Since they felt unappreciated by the San Francisco scouts, they were unwilling to give an inch in the argument or any other argument, no matter the subject.

In contrast to them, the laid-back San Francisco scouts who spent the last year studying and perfecting the secrets of tolerance and acceptance, were not that tolerant or willing to accept the Los Angeles scouts' rude reaction. They felt insulted and spoke their mind in raised voices, starting a heated argument that earned a place in the aliens' urban legends as the first ever recorded heated argument on the verge of the first ever fistfight, or more accurately, the first ever claw fight.

As I've told you before, we are very good in marketing and can easily influence even an alien, changing his way of life.

And what was the reason for all that commotion? What made the scouts almost duke it out? Well, it was a difference of opinion between the two teams about a critical subject. No, it wasn't about the Vietnam War, but of something much closer to their hearts. Yes, it was about Jimi Hendrix, or more specifically, about the way Jimi Hendrix used his teeth to play his guitar.

And it goes like this:

The Los Angeles scouts were adamant that Jimi was using his upper teeth, which were larger and stronger, while the San Francisco scouts insisted they, personally, saw Jimi using his lower teeth. They also emphasized that it's humanly impossible to play a guitar using your upper teeth as the large, weird-shaped human nose would always get in the way.

In an attempt to convince each other, the scouts started to imitate the way they believed Jimi was using his mouth to play his guitar. The spaceship's aisle was now occupied by a bunch of over-excited aliens jumping around, jamming imaginary guitars against their mouths, mimicking Jimi Hendrix, but it didn't stop there.

To better prove their point, each alien decided to mimic one of Jimi's greatest hits and now the spaceship's constrained space was filled with several loud and not so complimenting versions of Jimi's greatest creations. This commotion, which was a mix of the scouts' loud argument and out of tune music, grew louder and louder. It rolled along the spaceship aisle, reaching the spaceship's cockpit and the frustrated pilot inside it.

All he was trying to do was to find a way out of our solar system, to take his weird cargo back home. He never asked for their help, but didn't want any interruptions either. The loud sound, generated by the scouts, didn't help; on the contrary, it made his blood boil, especially considering the fact that he spent the last year confined to his spaceship.

If you were sitting in the empty co-pilot seat, you couldn't miss his disapproving facial expressions, the popping veins around his neck and the fiery look in his metallic eyes, but since you weren't there in the empty co-pilot seat, you missed it. The same goes for the scouts who were still shouting and arguing in the spaceship's belly.

What they didn't miss was the pilot's cold-as-ice voice over the spaceship's intercom. It was a chilling voice, completely foreign to the pilot's usual calm alien demeanor, broadcasting a short message, specifically intended for them. The pilot notified his over-excited passengers they had exactly one alien minute to return to their designated seats, strap on their seat belts and stay seated in a complete silence for the remainder of the trip. His chilling voice continued, promising the scouts that a failure to obey his orders may result in unforeseen misery as he, the pilot, would intentionally divert the spaceship and fly full throttle directly into that humongous planet in front of him, which he believed called

Neptune, and maybe then, he would be able to have some peace and quiet.

The scouts couldn't ignore the direct threat behind the icy voice and decided not to put the pilot to the test. With no other choice, they clutched their claws and complied with his demands. They rushed to their designated seats, strapped themselves in and sat quietly. Suddenly, the spaceship's belly was silent... too quiet, and completely noiseless; there was no sound or movement, nothing at all. Well sort of.

Afraid to move or speak, the still excited scouts were now again sitting, facing each other. Unhappy from their unfinished business, they resorted to the one thing they were still able to do. They started sticking their long tongues out, making faces at each other and they didn't stop for the rest of the trip.

They didn't move for the rest of the flight. They stayed in the same exact position as the pilot maneuvered the spaceship through our solar system. They didn't move an inch as he finally merged into our galaxy's highway and made a dash toward the moving Wormhole. They kept stationary in their seats as the spaceship zipped through the Wormhole and brought them back to the security of their galaxy. They didn't feel secure and wouldn't dare move a muscle.

Even as the spaceship approached their colony, slowed down and inched closer to its landing dock, the idea to unstrap themselves never crossed their minds. Finally, they were able to recognize the shape of the buildings below, but even that wasn't a good enough reason for them to risk their lives. The scouts stayed still, frozen in their seats, making not one sound, not one move – other than with their long tongues.

The spaceship used its boosters for the vertical landing and floated gradually toward its designated docking space. The scouts, who had been so terrified from the pilot's chilling message, became anxious. They couldn't trust the mindset of a pilot who was locked for a whole years in the constrained space of a sealed spaceship, at the corner of Haight and Ashbury. The way they saw it, it wasn't a good idea to challenge him or his sanity. Simply saying, they were still inside that floating spaceship above their planet surface and didn't want to give him any excuse to crash the spaceship into anything. They were certain that he might do so just for the heck of it, just to be done with them.

Only when the spaceship landed and shut down its engines, only then the scouts found their courage. Without waiting for the pilot to turn off the "Fasten Seat Belt" sign, they unbuckled themselves, jumped out of their seats and rushed to the nearest exit, trying to get as far as they could from the pilot's reach, just like us. As they were piling and pushing each other in the spaceship's narrow corridor, just like us, they were able to recognize the golden opportunity that had just presented itself. Mayhem filled that corridor as the scouts started elbowing each other intentionally, just like us. It was a perfect way for them to release all the anger they had accumulated during the "Quiet Time," forced on them by that unstable pilot. After all, now they had the perfect excuse, they could blame it on the limited space in that narrow corridor.

But there was an alternate motive for their dash to the spaceship's hatch. Each team wanted to be first to step out of the spaceship. They were certain there would be a ceremony waiting for them outside, a returning hero's welcome that involves speeches and medals. Each team wanted to be the first to accept the respect, congratulations and medals they believed they deserved.

Unfortunately for them, there was no ceremony outside the spaceship, no High Council representatives, no speeches, and definitely no medals. The spaceship's designated docking area was deserted with the exception of a lone alien who was waiting in that area's farthest corner. He also seemed to be grim and pretty much bored.

It was their supervisor, the same one who had sent them a year earlier on their mission. If it was his choice, he wouldn't be there either, but since he was their direct commander, he had no choice.

Now he had a front row seat to the sad spectacle that was unfolding in front of his very eyes. He was witnessing the returning scouts stumbling out of the spaceship's hatch in one big ball of mass made out of colorful clothing with the exception of purple legs and arms sticking out in all directions. The scouts, who were still dressed in human garments, slowly approached him, still pushing and elbowing each other. I'm sure that anyone else who watched such a sight would have laughed his head off, but not the supervisor. He was not amused.

That short distance, the scouts covered from the spaceship to the waiting supervisor, was sufficient enough to remind them that ceremonies, speeches and medals were Earth traditions, something they have picked up from one of our TV programs, and not a practice of their alien nation. That might have been the last wakeup call they needed to realize that "they were not in Kansas anymore." They were back home.

Still, they did their best to cut their losses and continued elbowing and pushing each other in their attempts, at a bare minimum, to be first to reach their supervisor, to be the first to hand him their respective reports. An uneasy feeling overcame the supervisor as he was witnessing the scouts' out-of-character conduct. It was the angst you feel when your gut tells you that no good can come out of this scenario. Unconsciously, the supervisor started to shake his head.

Chapter 5 – The Supervisor

Truthfully, the supervisor only cared about one thing and that was the scouts' reports. He didn't even care much about the reports as a whole, but just a single piece of information in them. He definitely, didn't care about the order in which they were delivered. Unable to understand the returning scouts' external appearance and strange manners made this need for knowledge more urgent. As a result, when the messy, sweating and hard breathing scouts finally stood in front of him, he snatched the reports from them before saying hello and searched for that piece of information. He was glancing quickly through the reports, reading their summaries when he found what he was looking for and realized that his concerns had just morphed into a real fear. Even though the two reports were written separately, the same exact conclusion was underlined in red in both reports, stating that those urgently needed replacement "Double AA" batteries were nowhere to be found and most probably didn't exist.

In his wildest dreams the supervisor never envisioned that after a yearlong mission to Earth the scouts would return empty handed. At a bare minimum, he had hoped to see a measly four-pack in their claws. To make things even worse, with every additional word he was reading the significance of the absent replacement batteries was growing bigger. A new crisis started to materialize in his mind that sent a shiver up his spine.

The reports painted a disturbing picture, describing those batteries as an illusion, a relic of the past that seized to exist. In the scouts' eyes, it was a lost cause, completely out of the aliens' reach, but it didn't stop there. The scouts went even further and recommended to relocate their whole colony closer to Earth. They actually had a place in mind as an optional new home, Saturn with its extraordinary rings. They hinted that its closeness to Earth made it a good candidate as it would allow them to acquire more up-to-date information about Jimi Hendrix's tour dates. They emphasized that such short distance would enable them to make weekend road trips to our planet at any given time with no advance planning and would relieve them of their dependence on those ever disappearing batteries. They also claimed that Saturn rings were just to cool to bypass as a contender.

The supervisor had to stop reading as he realized he was covered, head to toe, with cold sweat. He was worried of the unknown future – not the distant future, but the very near future. It was his responsibility to deliver the batteries or at a bare minimum the way to acquire them. He was so concerned about his own well-being that he did the bare minimum to acknowledge the scouts in a proper manner. He gave them one more glance, shook his head one more time, raised his hand and gave them the "Alien Welcome Home" salute before releasing them to their business. He was holding the two reports while watching the scouts walking away, still pushing and shoving each other. They disappeared behind the huge hanger and he also left, returning to his quarters, where he sat down and started a deeper examination of the two reports' content.

After spending a short time reading and comparing the two reports, he leaned back with a desperate look on his face. The more he read, the more confused he became. He didn't have to be a genius, which he wasn't, to recognize that the two reports completely contradicted each another.

His first clue was the two reports' distinctive and colorful language. The Los Angeles scouts' report reflected the Jive slang of the Sixties' black community and included words like "Bad-Ass," "Gimme Some Skin" and "Drop a Dime" while the San Francisco scouts' report was filled with phrases of the Sixties' flower children like "Far Out," "Bummed Out" and "Groovy." Those words, which were throughout the reports, made his work harder as he didn't understand their meaning. He wondered how it could be that two highly important reports, a reflection of a yearlong intelligence gathering, could be so hard to understand. And then it dawned on him. It wasn't just the reports' language that was so confusing, there was something else. The supervisor observed that during their time among what called "The Humans", the two scout teams had dealt with what seems to be not a single society, but two completely opposite societies. In his eyes it was fantastic and practically impossible. Any other alien world he ever encountered, including his own, was always composed of a single homogenous society and that's it. He continued reading the reports, trying to make sense of what seemed to him as a gaffe on the scouts' account.

While the Los Angeles team described a demanding society, confrontational and aggressive, the San Francisco team drew a picture of a peaceful, loving and accommodating society. Where the Los Angeles team suggested an aggressive, take no prisoners' invasion, the San Francisco team recommended an easygoing invasion, a calm approach that included an advance purchase of flowers in large quantities, preferably daisies. They claimed that it was the bare essential.

The Los Angeles scouts' report was grim and gave no hope to the human race, calling for its complete annihilation with the exception of the discriminated Black Panthers, Jimi Hendrix and his guitar collection. The San Francisco scouts' report drew a rosier picture of us, describing humans' love of life, laughter, rock and roll and some funny looking pills. It told the story of the Hippies' unconditional acceptance of the aliens, something that was emphasized in a form of a small memento, placed by the scouts on the report's cover. It was a peace sign made out of dry flowers. The report also mentioned the bond between Jimi and the Hippies, insisting that it would be a grave mistake to upset their idol with an act of aggression such as the Hippies complete annihilation. The scouts declared that such an act would affect his musical creativity. The report ended with the sentence "Make Love, Not War" printed in rainbow colors.

I must add that while on the spaceship, on their way home, when the Los Angeles scouts saw that memento, they added a big black fist and a short sentence to the cover of their report saying in bold black letters: "Power to the People."

Five seconds later, they **X**ed out the word "People" and replaced it with "Aliens." That made them feel better about themselves and lifted their tortured spirits for at least the next ten minutes.

There was the contradiction and the supervisor still couldn't understand how it is possible that two completely polarized societies were living beside each other on one planet. That was something unheard of. Never before, in any of their encounters of any planet and any galaxy, there were more than a single society occupying that space– never two!! And in all of those societies, all aliens were look alike, spoke alike, and thought alike.

I'm sure you can see why the supervisor was so confused. Think about it, this is even the way we perceive aliens existence or at least this is the way we portray them in our Sci-Fi books and movies. We always consider aliens as a single society, who look alike, speak alike and think alike. And if we think about them like that, why wouldn't the supervisor think about us in the same way?

Nevertheless, the supervisor had in front of him two reports, each describing a different society with a completely different state of mind. In his eyes, he could see only two reasons for that: either the scouts hadn't done their job or they had made a colossal mistake in their observations.

Either way he could come with only two conclusions: the first was that those reports were not to be trusted in their current condition and couldn't serve as the basis for a full-scale invasion of a faraway plant. The second was that he had to fix this situation ASAP as his neck was on the line.

The supervisor had never been the brightest bulb, but he was smart enough to know what buttons not to press. During his years in service, he had managed to advance through the ranks, successfully, to reach his current position. It wasn't on the sole merit of his intelligence, but by being an obedient, "Yes Man," oops, I meant, "Yes Alien." He hadn't mastered the art of getting out of trouble, but definitely knew how to avoid getting into it.

Now, beyond his control, he had stepped into one big mess. There was a major crisis on his hands and he had to resolve it without jeopardizing his current rank or position. In his eyes, the two reports were useless and didn't provide any real, concrete facts for the upcoming invasion. The lack of information about the much needed replacement batteries with the addition of the scouts' grim conclusions didn't help either.

The same questions that had been raised ahead of the scouting mission, about the batteries and the humans' planet still lingered. Those reports didn't meet his expectations from a yearlong mission, and wouldn't meet his superiors' expectations either. He had to devise a plan in which he would be able to deliver the bad news to the High Council, with a spin, and save his neck in the process. He had to figure out a way to make those reports presentable. He had to do so because there was no other choice and it had to be done pronto.

You see, just as the scouting mission was on its way, as the scouts' spaceship cleared the aliens' purple sky and was on its way to planet Earth, the addicted aliens were desperate for Jimi's music. They were looking for a temporary alternative solution, something to sustain their addiction until the scouts return with replacement "Double AA" batteries. Since they didn't have the equipment or the exact voltage, recharging the drained batteries was out of the question. Their next solution was more controversial. They collected their best engineers in an attempt to replicate those four-of-a-kind devices, an endeavor that turned into a disaster. While trying to investigate the batteries' internal content, acid spilled on one of their highly respected older engineers, who in return started screaming in high-pitched voice and running in circles in the crowded lab. This annoying spectacle didn't stop until he was granted a full week paid vacation and an assigned parking space, with his name, in front of their lab main entrance.

That fiasco convinced the aliens that there was no easy fix for the drained batteries crisis. They had to give up their attempts to re-create the illusive devices and left with no other option but to wait for the scouts return. They only left with the hope the scouts would bring a new stock of batteries or at least the knowledge about their whereabouts, something that would shape their invasion of Earth.

And then out of nowhere, like in the movies, our supervisor had an epiphany, a genius idea. Well, it seemed to be a genius idea at the time of its inception. He instructed to assemble their greatest musicians, against their will I must add, lock them in a soundproof room, and throw away the key. The musicians were told to perform Jimi's greatest hits nonstop, day and night, 24/7 for the next six months with an optional six months extension. He believed it was only a matter of time before the musicians could master playing Jimi's tunes. He was the one who, personally, diverted the planet wide intercom system cables from the dead Tape Player to this locked soundproof room. He considered it a temporary solution to compensate for the lack of the batteries and hoped it would elevate the aliens' spirit until the scouts return.

The last thing he had to do was to ease his superiors, the High Council members, concerns about copyright infringement and royalties. He had a solution for this as well. He told them that since no one but them, a nation of more than ten million aliens, know about those violations, as long as a nation of more than ten million aliens kept their mouth shut, no harm would be done. Considering their current situation, the High Council members were easy to convince.

Only a short time after this grand plan came to fruition, the aliens, and I do mean a nation of more than ten million aliens, comprehend that it wasn't such a genius idea but rather a dumb one. Their best musicians were unable to get even remotely close to Jimi's musical techniques. They did their best to imitate the greatest ten-fingered, guitar player of all times, but even above their lack of talent, how could they do so when all they had was four sharp claws? In a later interview with those musicians, they further admitted that the mere idea of anyone to believe in their capabilities to imitate Jimi's voice was even a dumber idea!

What came from that soundproof room didn't sound good at all. It wasn't the music the aliens were accustomed to, the music their musicians had mastered and it, definitely, wasn't Jimi Hendrix music. It stunk. It was more like a constant string of painful loud sounds mixed with the musicians' squeaky voices. And now that horrible screeching sound was playing nonstop, day and night, 24/7 all over the purple aliens' colony and the key to that soundproof room was nowhere to be found.

And what was the end result? Well, it resulted in an alien nation, more than ten million strong, who had to listen to this painful and constant loud noise nonstop, day and night, 24/7, causing all of them major headaches. The supervisor's plan backfired and he was confronted by a whole nation of upset aliens, complaining and demanding his head. To be accurate, it was the whole alien nation minus one, his wife who knew him better than any of them and loved him unconditionally.

Since, he was the architect of the scouts' six months mission, he waited, anxiously, for their return. He was hopping to save his skin and keep his good standing in the colony. By now it wasn't that great and became worse, when the scouts delayed their return with the mission extension of an additional six months.

Now, if there was ever a word to describe something worse than worse I would use it to describe the supervisor's mental condition, when he realized that the scouts had returned empty-handed (empty-clawed?).

And to add fuel to the fire, they also returned with useless reports, reflecting a lost year and a complete waste of time and resources. Those reports couldn't give him a clear idea how to mobilize the aliens' mightiest army. Now it was on him. He had to construct the plans to invade a faraway planet that might not even possess the key for the highly required batteries. And to make things worse, he had to do devise those plans, ignoring the remote possibility that this faraway planet might really be the host of two opposite yet completely crazy societies.

That one long year, which was filled with ongoing grumbling from his fellow aliens made sure to give him a constant headache, but his scouts' actions on planet Earth upgraded this headache into a perfect migraine. He had to make it stop, to find a solution, to find a way to save the essential invasion and his skin.

Dissecting the problem on hand, braking it to little pieces, trying to find an answer – all of that led him to one solution, his best recourse. He decided to splice the two reports together and combine them into one. With some contribution of his own imagination, he will create an alternate report, a botched one. He started by reading both reports thoroughly and then read them a few more times. For someone who lived among more than ten million aliens, all of whom looked alike, spoke alike, and thought alike, it was easy for the supervisor to convince himself the scouts were wrong. There was no way that two contradicting societies somehow succeeded to live on the same space in the same planet.

He firmly ruled it was a mistake and that most likely, the scouts just observed the same society differently.

His second conclusion was much easier to ascertain. While on planet Earth, the scouts had the time of their lives and their greatest success was their ability to blend with the humans. But that was where it ended and from that point forward the rest of their information was wrong.

He, for one, couldn't understand the meaning of the events, described in the reports. It was obvious the scouts had an even greater time whenever they attended Jimi's live shows or spent time with him backstage, whatever backstage meant.

One might say he was jealous of the scouts, but regardless of his personal feelings he knew those reports couldn't justify a year's worth of intelligence gathering, and that he would have to be very creative, very quickly.

You see, the way he saw that, there was a line in the sand, never to be crossed. Crossing this line meant jeopardizing all he had worked for, his professional achievements, present rank and any possibility of future promotions. In their original format, the two colorful and useless reports clearly crossed that line and left him with no other choice, but to do whatever was required to rectify this situation.

I can tell you of another time where the supervisor, in his younger form, had to deal with that same line. In that earlier time the line was crossed so badly that, even today, the supervisor cannot understand how he was able to save his skin.

It all started when a meteorite shower approached the aliens' planet, which was always in the path of something moving through space. This time it was this meteorite shower. Suddenly, a very large meteorite broke away from the pack, changed direction and started heading on a collision course with the aliens' colony. Should it crash into the planet surface, it would most likely wipe out this whole alien nation, but the aliens were prepared for such events. They had the tools to deal with very large meteorites that just broke off from the pack and were on collision course with their planet surface. It was a state-of-the-art missile system that protected them from their dangerous skies, capable of tracking incoming objects, calculating their route and targeting them for immediate destruction. It was a very expensive and advanced system, but it had a small flaw. For one stupid reason or another, it required the controller's intervention, an alien touch, to launch those intercepting missiles.

This meant that a missile launch could only occur if the alien, sitting in front of the large control panel, pressed the big red button in the middle of that console. Yes, it was a great control panel with lights, sounds and gauges that handled absolutely everything except for the most important part, the launch of the intercepting missiles.

On that particular night, it just happened that the alien behind the great control panel was our supervisor, in his younger form. Unfortunately, when the large meteorite broke off from the pack and changed course, our supervisor was too busy with some personal matters. To be precise, he was updating his status on the intergalactic social network with some pictures of his last vacation. He was doing so while chatting with a six eyed, bright orange female alien he had met online and with whom he was hoping for a meaningful relationship. In other words, every ounce of his attention was occupied and he was completely ignoring the control panel's large screen, which by now had captured the large incoming meteorite that was growing closer and closer.

Maybe it was an instinct, but at the last moment his eyes glimpsed at the large screen and, to his horror, saw the imminent danger. Yes, by now that incoming large meteorite was, definitely, in sight. It was so close that it covered the entire large screen.

Since it was that close, the young supervisor knew it was too late and too dangerous to press the big red button and deploy the intercepting missiles. He had to make a spur of the moment decision, to implement the best solution he could think of and he did. First, he urgently yet politely ended his chat with the bright orange female alien, swearing to her that in his current condition he really, really hoped to meet her one day as long as his future allowed it.

His next action was to crawl under that great console, cover his pointy ears and position himself in the alien fetal position. Lastly, he closed his eyes and waited for the inevitable big "Boom."

A few seconds later, came that big "Boom," a very big "Boom." Even with his ears covered, he heard this huge "Boom" and then nothing else – it was quiet. Since he didn't see his life flashing before his eyes or felt anything else, he became confused. He only knew that he was alive, shaking from fear, in the alien fetal position under that great control panel, but alive. He waited a few more seconds with his eyes closed, just in case there was a delay and his whole life would decide to flash before his eyes. Since that didn't happen he opened his eyes.

He crawled from under the great console, stood up and looked around him. Everything was intact, nothing broken, damaged or destroyed. He rushed to the great control panel for additional information and became more confused. None of the counter-measures had been deployed, but the large screen was clear again with no sign of that large meteorite.

"What, in the hell, just happened?" he thought to himself, trying to make sense of the events. A short time later it came to him. His whole planet and the purple population on it had been saved by pure luck. The catastrophe was averted not by the aliens' advanced missile system, but by another meteorite of a smaller size. This meteorite decided to change direction as well and be on a direct collision course with the larger meteorite. By all accounts, it was a miracle as the smaller meteorite collided with the larger one, altering both meteorites' courses and destroying the large meteorite in the process, seconds before it would crash into the aliens' planet.

No one but the young supervisor knew the tale of the two meteorites. Right there and then, the young supervisor pledged that no one but him should ever know about this disaster "that never happened", including the six eyed bright orange female alien, with which he tied the knot, right after that incident.

Standing before the High Council members, trying to explain that huge "boom" in their skies, the young supervisor explained the elders it was the result of a secret general rehearsal for the surprise fireworks show, which was planned for the upcoming aliens' "Independence Day" celebrations. The elders, who were rattled by that big "boom," became thrilled with his explanation and kindly asked him to reserve the front row seats for them at the time of the celebrations. They were so impressed with that "secret" rehearsal and couldn't wait to see the real show.

Can you comprehend how much effort, money and time the young supervisor exerted, traveling to every store on his planet and neighboring planets, on a mission to purchase any available fireworks just to replicate that same big "Boom" during the aliens' "Independence Day" fireworks show?

On a good note, the young supervisor made sure to immediately alter the aliens' defense system, removing the big red button from the great control panel and automating the launch of the intercepting missiles.

That fateful day left a lasting impression in the supervisor's mind, always reminding him how lucky he was to find enough fireworks. This time he was determined not to depend on his luck. Simply saying, the supervisor knew that this time there weren't enough fireworks in all the galaxies combined to outperform this big "BOOM."

There was no way to justify the reports' content. Delivering them, in their current condition, to the High Council was out of the question. Since he was scheduled to present his report the very next day, there was no time to spare. It was his duty to provide them with the information required to formulate the plans and objectives of the future invasion and it couldn't be done with the information on hand. On such short notice, combining the two human societies into one was the best course of action. So he would combine the two reports into one and create a whole new report with a whole new and consistent human society, made out of details he could incorporate from both reports.

After all, he was thinking to himself, the High Council elders had never met a human and wouldn't know the difference. He would shuffle the two reports and add his own touch, erasing the confusion of the unthinkable, two societies and their completely opposite conduct. His creation would remove this confusion, while creating a new one in the elders' minds. He needed this kind of confusion during his presentation. It would subdue the elders and reduce the chance of more grueling questions.

He went to work and a few hours later had the new report before him. This report told an intriguing yet incorrect story about us, made out of facts that introduced our society as an unstable one. In this modified report, we were literally a society that was black and white without a middle ground. Humans were upset while happy, calm with a short temper, accommodating while aggressive and above all, had no fashion skills whatsoever, something that was easy to prove based on our choice of clothing. Was there any other way to describe a human wearing a black beret and tie-dyed T-Shirts on a sunny day? That was considered a bad choice of clothing even in their world.

The hard part was done and the only thing left was to put on the finishing touches, which were the report's cover and the supervisor's recommendations. As for the cover, the supervisor removed the dry flowers and the drawing of the human fist. Instead he inserted a clean cover with a single sentence:

"Make Love or War, Whatever floats your spaceship."

The cover was done. It was now time for the supervisor to add his personal analysis and the invasion's objectives. That was when he started to have doubts, wondering whether there was a slim chance that the scouts were right? Could it be that there were two human societies on the same planet, and was it possible that there were no batteries waiting for them at the time of the invasion?

He wasn't sure what to think. After all, there were two leftover batteries, on display in their colony square, which he saw everyday on his way to work – those were not figures of his imagination. Those batteries were real!

Even as he was attributing the scouts' conclusions to their laziness and sense of pride, he was concerned how to justify this expensive, large-scale invasion if there were no batteries? Had he missed anything? Was there any other alternative to explore ahead of this invasion? The supervisor was looking for answers and decided to find them in the invasion's future objectives, where he would define the aliens' highest expectations from this future invasion. Everything would be obvious from the beginning, including a failure in the quest for the replacement batteries. And then it came to him. He decided to go one step further and construct an alternative scenario, an additional objective that might solve the replacement batteries issue once and for all.

The more he thought about it, the more it made sense. Understanding the nature of this alternative scenario, he couldn't foresee the High Council's reaction to it, but still believed that it was worth a shot. Altogether, he was able to come with three recommendations, which he added to his modified report.

The first was related to the pilot's personal account of Earth's parking difficulties. The supervisor recommended abandoning landing the much larger spaceships on Earth, leaving them orbiting in outer space, eliminating those parking issues altogether. He justified it by the crazy human society's reaction to large, armed spaceships hovering for days over their skies, in a tedious search for parking. He also mentioned the risk of cosmetic damage to those large spaceships should they try to park in a tight spot. He emphasized that leaving those spaceships in outer space would allow the invading aliens to maintain the element of surprise.

His next recommendation was based on his impression of the returning scouts. You see, the supervisor couldn't understand why they had returned so cheerfully from what he considered to be a failed mission. Why were they so excited about this remote insignificant planet called Earth? In his eyes, this planet was a primitive place that, by all accounts, seemed to have an identity crises and couldn't even make a simple decision about the nature of its own society? Since the scouts' transformation was a mystery to him, he recommended to execute the invasion with no expectations. He wanted to secure an opening for either invasion's outcome, success or failure. He hoped that by lowering those expectations, even a failed invasion would be acceptable, something like a "No Harm, No Foul" invasion that wouldn't jeopardize his position.

Finally, it was the time for his third and last recommendation, his own creation that will be remembered for generations to come as "The Third Secretive Objective." He based the premise of this objective on remarks he had found in both reports. In his eyes, it was the last resort and maybe the only solution to the replacement "Double AA" batteries crisis. But it wasn't that simple as there were lots of rules and guidelines to follow. Being aware of the aliens' bureaucracy, he knew that two years should be a sufficient amount of time for this objective to be processed through the aliens' red tape and be ready to unleash in case of emergency. Regardless of that, and without waiting for the High Council's approval, the supervisor initiated a secret and new construction project.

Doing things behind your superiors' back is not a smart idea, especially when you are spending so many funds on a huge new structure that would be erected right smack in the center of this purple colony. Sooner or later they would observe this structure and start asking questions, but as I said before, this supervisor wasn't the smartest alien and since ignorance is bliss he covered his ignorance with confidence. Yes, he was very confident while crafting the botched report and even more confident about the new report's objectives, including his "Third Secretive Objective" and the huge new structure.

But as he finished working on the report, his confidence level plummeted and he was overcome with a heavy sense of insecurity, an uneasy feeling, the beginning of an anxiety attack. It was the realization that the easy part of the process was done and the more complicated part was about to begin, the delivery of the report to the High Council members.

It wasn't the false report that worried him and it wasn't even the endless amount of rubber stamps he had to collect from the High Council building's security team that scared him. It was the actual High Council building's security team members that rattled him to his core. What horrified him was the knowledge of the mental and physical abuse he was about to endure from this security team.

Chapter 6 – The High Council Building Security Team

What can I tell you about the High Council building's security team members? Well, if we put aside the fact that they were purple aliens, at first glance they were no different from any other security team you'd meet in any lobby of any building, at least in the first year of their employment.

They seemed to be a bunch of friendly aliens who were assigned to maintain the security of the aliens' Command and Control Center, where the High Council elders resided. For years, they did their job as efficiently as could be, but as time progressed they became quite bored with the traditional and routine security procedures so they decided to spice it up a notch or two ...or ten. Simply stated, they decided to abandon the comfort behind the lobby's counter and become more proactive with every incoming visitor, implementing new "enhanced" security procedures in the process. Those new procedures were of their own creation and allowed them to be much more interactive and intrusive with each new visitor to the building.

While visiting the building, you would have to go through them on your way to the floor of your destination. They would make sure you'll go through hell and do so with a friendly smile on their faces. But the supervisor had no choice. He had to meet the

High Council elders and to do so he had to go through the friendly members of the Command and Control building's security team.

The aliens' High Council was the aliens' highest authority and was made from a group of six elder aliens who kept themselves isolated in a secluded area. It was at the farthest corner of the fifth and highest floor of the main building, located in the heart of the aliens' Command and Control Center. Truthfully, the aliens had no need for any kind of security team to protect the elders or the Command and Control Center. They had no internal or external threats that required such an organized and methodical security team. The true foundations for the team's creation were the job security it provided, the great benefits, and the sharp-looking uniforms with the shiny buttons. Yes, those aliens just looked so good in uniforms.

Can you understand the multilevel security that encompassed the Command and Control Center? Those security teams were everywhere and, needless to say, most of them were in the building itself. It was jam-packed with security teams, located in the lobby and on each of the building's five floors. Therefore, on your way to meet the High Council members you would have to pass through five highly trained security teams and five levels of scrutiny, at a bare minimum. Since those teams were proficient in the art of verbal offensiveness and physical abuse, it was a given that upon arrival to the fifth floor, you would become half the alien you used to be before this humiliating process.

And it was all done in the name of security. At least that's what they stated, never apologizing for their conduct as they always explained with a smile that:

"They were only doing their job, and if they did not do their job, they would be reported to someone, not sure exactly who it was and for that reason they cannot give you his name or any other information where to lodge a complaint."

It was a bunch of Mumbo Jumbo.

This security process was misleading from the get go. Arriving at the building's lobby, you would be greeted by the very friendly and smiling members of the security team. They would engage you with some small talk about the weather while checking your identity. Still smiling they would instruct you to use the stairs, insisting the elevators were out of order and that they were waiting for the repair alien. Truthfully, the only reason the repair alien never showed up was that, like everyone else, he was doing his best to stay away from the claws of the security team members.

Unaware, you'll thank them and start your way to the next level, only to realize the radical change a single flight of stairs can make. Now there were no more smiles and the security team members were all business. They would take you through additional screening, checking your briefcase, your height, weight, dental records, and more endless questions. And the process would only escalate with every flight of stairs you climb, a mix of physical and intrusive checks, involving explicit body searches, machinery, and latex gloves, which out of respect I'd rather not elaborate any further.

Every so often, there will be an alien who had passed all of the security checkpoints and reached the fifth floor, just to realize that he had left his briefcase in the trunk of his parking hovercraft. This alien would be out of luck as he would gain no sympathy from the security team members and would have to start the same security process all over again with one small difference. This time around, the same security team members in the lobby would greet him with much bigger smiles, or more accurately, bigger grins.

But if you were lucky enough not to forget your belongings and passed all security teams checkpoints, you would find yourself on the building's fifth and last floor. You just earned the right to meet the High Council elders and to receive a coupon for the aliens' army outlet store, where you could purchase a new set of uniforms to replace the one you were wearing before the security process, which most likely were shredded to pieces during this procedure. A second coupon would be provided for the purchase of a baby pacifier, to ease the long, sleepless, and uneasy night you are about to endure while recovering from the unpleasant encounter with the security team members in the High Council's Command and Control Center building. After all, even an alien cannot suck on a claw. It is just too dangerous.

Our supervisor had to meet the High Council members. That was the first thing that went through his mind when he opened his eyes the next morning. He was still sitting on his bed, collecting his thoughts, taking a good look at his custom-fitted uniform hanging in the far corner of the room. It would be the last time he would see it in such great condition as it certainly wouldn't survive the day ahead. He stood up and dressed slowly, spending some time in solitude. Only then he left the room, searching for his alien wife. She was in the guest bedroom, preparing it for her husband's return, aware of the long and painful day ahead of him. She was getting ready for this miserable night, and as much as she cared for her husband's wellbeing, she didn't see any reason for her to lose sleep as well.

He kissed her alien forehead, took his briefcase and hopped into his hovercraft. He flew quietly, navigating his way to the alien Command and Control Center building.

The elders were waiting for the supervisor's arrival. Having years of experience they knew that just waiting can be a real waste of time so they had found a more constructive way to pass their time. They were placing bets on the number of times he would have to go through the security teams' screening process on his way to their secluded area at the farthest corner of the fifth floor.

Meanwhile the supervisor reached the building and parked his hovercraft. He stepped into the building's lobby and was greeted with the expected "Good Morning" by the friendly and smiling security team members as they were putting latex gloves on. He passed that checkpoint and with an uneasy feeling stepped into the building's staircase, unable to ignore the grin on their faces.

Two hours later he emerged out of the staircase onto the fifth floor. He wasn't standing, but on his knees, crawling, covered with sweat and a torn uniform. As he was dragging himself through the hallway to the farthest and secluded corner of the fifth floor, a thought was passing through his mind: "Why can't the elders just wait for me closer to the staircase?"

He reached their quarters, pushed the door open and crawled to the center of the room. With his last ounce of strength, he raised his body and stood on his feet only to find himself facing the six elder aliens of the aliens' High Council.

They were sitting behind a long metal console on a raised platform, quietly staring at him. The room's only source of light came from behind them. It was a dim, dark purple ambiance meant to illuminate only one side of the elders' faces, keeping the rest of their facial features in the shadows. It wasn't a coincidence but planned in advance, a way for the elders to intimidate their guests. They were very much involved in the construction of their quarters, creating dramatic surroundings to keep whoever was before them on their toes. As I told you before, this alien nation was made out of jokers and their elders were no different.

The supervisor was standing, breathing hard, doing his best to stay calm as they stared at him, quiet and somber. The room was filled with a thick silence and then, without warning, the elders turned to each other and began settling their bets, ignoring him altogether. And what did the supervisor do, you ask? Well, he had no choice but to try to continue standing tall and wait patiently.

The elders finished their doings, leaned back in their chairs, and turned their full attention back to the supervisor. Now, they were ready for his presentation about the yearlong scouting mission and the search for the small power sources. As with the rest of the aliens they were in desperate need to have that human device, the Tape Player, functioning again, playing Jimi Hendrix's music. But unlike the rest of the aliens, they had the right to be the first in line to receive the supervisor's report of the scouting mission's outcome.

In fact, the elders were no different than the rest of the aliens and, like them, they became addicted to Jimi's music. Since they were the "Aliens in Charge," they were able to do as they pleased and during the early stage of their growing addiction, they used their authority. The elders ordered an immediate reconfiguration of their planet-wide sound system, which was an expensive and unneeded re-cabling project of the fairly new and up-to-date existing sound system.

The project specified rerouting of the first audio cable that came out from the humans' device to the rest of the colony. The elders ordered that specific cable to be routed to their secluded space in the farthest corner of the fifth floor in the main building located in the Command and Control Center area before it was distributed to the rest of the aliens' planet.

They had a good reason to do so. You see, they wanted to be the first in line to enjoy Jimi's enchanting music. They assumed having this direct connection to the device's output would give them a better music experience, higher fidelity, and no sound quality loss. It seems that regardless of their advanced technology, the elders never heard about the speed of sound.

But truth be told, the elders weren't engineers, they were politicians and like any other politicians, even alien politicians, they never passed on an opportunity to bend the rules to their advantage. On any occasion that they misused their authority, there was a logical justification. One time it was out of necessity and another time it was an emergency. In rare situations they even justified their doing it as a way to avert a disaster. Now, it was Jimi Hendrix's music at stake and if that was not a necessity turned into emergency on the verge of a disaster, then what was?

Like the rest of the aliens, the elders were caught by surprise when the batteries drained. As leaders, it was their responsibility to come up with a solution and after an emergency meeting, they agreed unanimously to dispatch the scouting mission to Earth. They were no fools and after reviewing their neighbors' information, they knew that even an innocent visit to our planet could turn into an adventure.

Their neighbors recalled tranquil and starry nights in one of Earth's forests, which in a split second transformed into a chaotic venture, disrupted by a large group of humans who normally appeared just before bedtime. The humans, dressed in green uniforms and metal cooking pots on their heads, would come equipped with bright beams of light, and if that wasn't enough, they just wouldn't keep quiet. They would make so much noise, destroying this peaceful night, leaving you with no other option but to stand up, look around, and try to figure out what they were looking for and why they were so loud? What could they be searching for, in such a remote forest, in the middle of the night?

The neighbors told the elders that most likely the humans had lost something. Was there any other reason for them to point their bright beams of light in all directions and shout to one another: "Do you see anything?"

The neighbors continued saying that since they had already lost their good night's sleep, they might as well try to help the humans. And the best they could do was to shout back to the humans, "No, we don't see anything," hoping the humans would give up their search, leave the forest and let them have that good night's sleep.

Their neighbors told them that what happened next was even more frustrating. It seems that with each of their responses, more humans would show up equipped with more disturbing bright beams of lights, making even more noise. This ongoing commotion infringed upon that good night's sleep and left them with no other choice, but to pack their equipment and vanish from the planet surface. They added that being so tired and upset with the inconsiderate humans, convinced them that crossing path with them would be a bad idea. So they made their departure up in a straight line as far and as fast as they could. The neighbors ended their story, saying that they left with no other option, but to spend the night on the much cooler and uncomfortable red planet nearby.

Upon hearing that, the elders decided to send the scouts on a six months scouting mission with an optional six months extension. They assumed that it was a reasonable amount of time for the scouts to get at least one night's sleep with no interference from the humans. In all fairness, they also believed that it was the most time they could survive listening to Jimi's music performed by their best musicians.

A few days into the scouting mission, they realized the magnitude of their mistake. They couldn't tolerate the horrible music coming from the soundproof room for even a second more. When they were informed of the scouts' delayed return, for an additional six months, they grew desperate for the replacement batteries. When they heard about the scouts return, they were thrilled, but on the next day, when they realized that the dreadful music of their musicians was still "On Air," they suspected something had gone terribly wrong so they summoned the supervisor to appear before them.

They had some very important questions for the supervisor. They wanted to know if there was a valid reason for the mission's extension. They were curious what went through the scouts minds as it didn't seem they wanted to return home. They, definitely, wanted to know why there were still no replacement "Double AA" batteries.

But most important, they needed to know: Where in the hell was the "OFF" button that would shut down this damn sound system and stop the horrific music played by their greatest musicians?

The elders had never seen "Made in California, USA - Double AA Batteries" before and wondered what made those precious items so difficult to obtain. They hoped that the scout's mission would shed some light on this mystery. Above all, they were perplexed regarding the reasons that these living organisms named "humans" would be so bold as to send a teaser called a "Time Capsule" to their neighbors in a faraway galaxy? Why would anyone go through the trouble of stuffing this device with so many things for the sole purpose of showing off, only to refuse to take the credit for it? They started to think that maybe the use of force was the only way for them to put their claws on those power source units.

Since they suspected the scouts had returned without batteries, the elders wanted to speak with the supervisor to start figuring out numbers. They wanted to know the amount of spaceships, quantity of supplies, and size of the invasion force they would need to acquire those units they later learned to call: "Made in California, USA - Double AA batteries."

This urgent need for replacement batteries kept them preoccupied, but it wasn't the only thing on their minds. Like the rest of the aliens, they were thirsty for any bit of information about their idol, Jimi Hendrix. What was he up to during that past year? Was he the real thing? And had he produced any new music?

Anxious to hear the supervisor's presentation, they gave him a few moments to catch his breath. The supervisor took a deep breath and started his presentation while watching the elders gently leaning back in their comfortable chairs, closing their metallic eyes and concentrating on his voice. But that didn't last for long.

A few minutes after, their closed eyes were open again, their aliens' ears were raised and that comfortable position, I've told you about, was forgotten. The elders were leaning forward, looking at him with an expression of disbelief on their faces, the unmistakable expression of total loss. They weren't sure how to digest the supervisor's information.

It was the supervisor's own report, the combination of the scouts' reports and it didn't praise the human race nor shed true light on its ways. Again, it wasn't a flattering report as it presented us as a confused race who suffered from "Dissociative Identity Disorder," a multi-personality disorder. It painted a picture of a race that was in a constant fight with itself and as a result would shift without warning across the two extremes of the emotional scale. We could be nice and friendly at one moment and upset and aggressive in the next, but it didn't stop there. The supervisor continued to describe us as an innovative, free-spirited society with a spark for life, a society that believed in a brighter future while at the same time we were a depressed and unhappy society who had lost the spark for life and had no hope about their future.

The supervisor ignored the elders' facial expressions and continued his presentation, moving without hesitation to present his recommendations. By than the elders had a better picture, incorrect though, about the life forms that stood between them and the replacement "Double AA" batteries. In their mind we were a peace-loving society that was willing to use any means at our disposal, including violence, to achieve the peace we were longing for. They believed that since we had no problem whatsoever to go across oceans to Vietnam with guns in our hands in search for that peace, we would have no problem to maybe even go across galaxies for that same reason. To say the least, for the elders it was a captivating yet scary concept at the same time.

By now, they had an established opinion about us. Humans were a weird race, the kind they'd never met before, and as we all know, weird is just another word for unstable – and unstable is just one way to describe dangerous and everyone knows that it is important to stay away from anything dangerous.

The elders' logic wasn't any different than ours. The supervisor's botched report only enhanced the magnitude of their problem. The last thing they wanted was to approach such a controversial and dangerous race as ours. If they didn't need those precious replacement batteries, they would have left us alone on our planet, in our solar system, in our galaxy and wouldn't have stepped into this puddle of quicksand, but they had no choice.

The reality was that they needed those batteries badly and had to go through us to get them.

The supervisor was describing the invasion objectives, starting with the first two objectives, which were accepted by the elders without a question. Then he paused for a moment, took a deep breath, and went on to describe his last objective, the "Third Secretive Objective." That was when the room became quieter as the elders grew wary. They were not sure if they liked it or not. It wasn't only for the expense and logistics involved, but much more than that. Approving this "Third Secretive Objective" meant ignoring every rule in the universe and that was a hard decision to make. It was a hard decision, but they were desperate.

They were addicted and needed those replacement batteries, so they decided to compromise and keep this objective viable, to be executed only in case of emergency if all other options had failed.

As the elders digested the supervisor's report, measuring its value, they started to consider all the "Pros," which was only one – the replacement batteries – and all the "Cons," which were a lot.

But regardless of their tally, a decision was made to continue with the invasion plans with one small change. Based on that fraudulent report's description of us, the aliens altered the invasion's original plans and added a new angle.

This would be the first time ever for this alien nation to invade a planet with no weapons. Since they became so concerned about the humans' reaction to any unexpected aggression, the elders decided to eliminate the use of force in the initial stages of the invasion, essentially to eliminate an armed invasion. The aliens were afraid of scaring us in the process of their invasion.

After the presentation came to its end, the elders summoned their generals and instructed them to come up with a new training program for their army. They ordered them to prepare their army for a future invasion of a remote planet in a remote galaxy. Their army was to take over a weird, unstable, and dangerous society that had been introduced to them through a completely misleading report. The generals had to figure out a way to invade our planet with no weapons or spaceships in a surprise move. Those invading forces had to survive on our planet surface on their own until they were able to secure a sufficient amount of parking spaces. That one small change turned the army's preparation into a complex task.

The generals, themselves, had to change their mindsets before applying those changes to their subordinates. They had to abandon all of their traditional invasion tactics and come up with new ones, which they were supposed to relay to their foot soldiers.

Their first order to their troops was to discard their existing army training manuals, simply saying – throw them out the windows. In those days, everywhere you went, you could see young alien soldiers throwing their military training books out the windows.

Well, those heavy books almost made it through the windows. All of them went as far as the specially made, sealed, protective glass windows allowed them, only to bounce back and hit the young alien soldiers right on their foreheads. It is more accurate to say that in those days everywhere you went you could see young alien soldiers walking around with a red spot on their foreheads. Only then could the generals start implementing their new tactics, the same tactics they planned to use at the time of the future invasion of Earth, the same invasion that never happened.

It wasn't an easy change for the alien soldiers, who up to this point were used to invading with all of their might, kicking the front door down. Now they had to depart from their aggression, and more important, from their weapons. Those alien soldiers loved their laser ray guns, their shiny spaceships and all of those plasma explosions, but all of it was taken away from them.

Hands down, it was a different kind of training, in which the alien generals created a group of friendly, easygoing purple aliens able to transform, in a matter of seconds, into unhappy and belligerent creatures. Their new army was made of strong minded, goal-driven aliens, yet easy to convince to forget their goals if handed flowers or a roll of that good stuff. Most important, this new army became proficient in the art of complaining and gladly accepted invitations for any protest or spontaneous party under starry skies, especially parties that involved Jimi's tunes and some of those gooey homemade special brownies.

The pilot's detailed description about Earth's impossible parking conditions forced the aliens to rework the logistics for their army's transportation to our planet's surface. The aliens had to figure out an inexpensive way to transfer their army, twenty thousand strong, to Earth's surface. I am sure you aware that energy is an expensive commodity and at times can be in scarce supply. Well, it wasn't any different in the aliens' world. Whether it was Earth's crude oil or the aliens' special energy mix, that concern of waste was always there and the aliens had their concerns as well.

Taking the pilot's input into consideration, the aliens assumed that they would encounter the same parking issues and frustrations. They didn't care to start their invasion hovering for days above their targets, wasting energy in an endless search for good parking spots. No good could come out of that other than wasted time and, literally, energy. They were also concerned about their newly trained army morale. By now, that new army they created had very short tempers and didn't care for long trips or unexplained delays.

The generals knew that low morale wouldn't lend itself to great results and decided to eliminate weapons and spaceships during their approach to Earth. They simply didn't want to jeopardize their quest for the replacement batteries. They would park the large transportation spaceships in outer space and initiate their landing with an "All Clear" signal from the invading forces' communication officers, confirming that a sufficient amount of parking spaces had been secured.

In their new invasion plans, the same generals would lead the invading forces and situate themselves on Earth's surface.

They would proceed to secure large parking spots, mostly made out of multiple parking spaces in Wal-Mart's parking lots, not by force, but with the support of the aliens' translation team members. That was an exclusive group of aliens who had spent the last two years perfecting their knowledge of the English language. They would occupy those empty parking spots and with their slick tongues, prevent humans from parking, giving them lame excuses. They would say that they were keeping those spots for their wives who were just a moment away. Only then would the aliens' communication officers transmit the agreed signal, initiating the large spaceships' landing in those designated spaces. The spaceships' pilots had to make sure not to damage any of the humans' automobiles during the landing process. You see, the last thing the aliens wanted was to deal with upset car owners or devious insurance company representatives upon their arrival. A successful landing would allow the delivery of supplies, weapons and additional equipment to the ground forces and mark the beginning of the invasion's second stage.

That was a controversial plan. Who in his right mind would invade a planet with no weapons or transportation, only to maintain the element of surprise? How can you transport anything to a plant's surface if you are planning on leaving your transportation spaceships in outer space? But the biggest question of all was how can anyone transfer an alien army, twenty thousand strong, from outer space to Earth's surface, completely unnoticed?

It was a great question that came with a questionable answer. The aliens' best solution was to literally drop in on us. What I mean is that it was the aliens' decision to come in as drops, raindrops to be more accurate. Drop after drop after drop.

As crazy as it sounds, the aliens who envisioned a surprise attack on our planet and eliminate the use of their war machines were contemplating for days how to achieve this stealth maneuver? What could they possibly use instead? As they were kicking around that problem, they were approached by their top scientists who informed them that they had a solution. The scientists introduced the curious elders and generals to their latest and greatest innovation in matter transportation, something they enjoyed calling "The Drop Process."

And indeed, it was an exciting concept in which organic matter was converted into liquid matter at the point of origin to disappear into the belly of the scientists' new machine. And then out of nowhere, the same liquid matter would reappear as drops at a specified destination and reassemble back into the same living, breathing organic matter it was at the point of origin. The scientists insisted that the procedure would work flawlessly as long as no one interrupted the process and that every drop, <u>not one less</u>, reached its destination.

The scientists even prepared a demonstration. They used this "Drop Method" on an alien frog, which was more or less the size of an Earth frog, transporting it from their lab directly to the center of the alien army's mess hall, where the aliens' top soldiers, their "Special Forces" team, were in the midst of having lunch. The frog just reappeared on one of the dining tables occupied by those brave soldiers. The elders and generals were very impressed by the successful transportation, but were not impressed at all from the commotion and panicked screams of their soldiers from that elite unit.

This successful demonstration was what the elders and generals were hoping for and enabled them to reach a decision right then and there. They would use this transportation method at the time of Earth's future invasion. Their army, twenty thousand strong, would drop onto Earth in a quiet, unexciting and casual way, keeping the element of surprise, eliminating the intimidation factor, and taking over the human race. In their eyes, it was the edge they were looking for to have a better shot in getting replacement "Double AA" batteries.

But there was one small detail their scientists failed to mention, something they considered an irrelevant detail. Since there was not one alien who was willing or crazy enough to volunteer to go through this "Drop Process," they had never tested that method on a full-grown alien and always used alien frogs, who on their part - never protested. Later the scientists would justify their silence, telling everyone that since no one asked, they had no reason to say anything.

So it happened that at the beginning of 1970 the aliens' High Council elders gave their generals the green light to board, along with their soldiers, the humongous transportation spaceships and initiate the first stage of the invasion that never happened.

Chapter 7 – The Drop Process

It started on a beautiful sunny day in early spring of 1970. Dark purple slimy drops were falling over the cities of Los Angeles and San Francisco. At first glance, it looked as if the drops were falling randomly, but a careful inspection would reveal that there was a methodical pattern involved. The drops were only falling in specific locations, like they were chosen in advance and it wasn't the two cities' main squares, monuments or major gathering spots. For no apparent reason, the locations were the cities' dark alleys, the ones behind the little mom-and-pop shops, located in both cities small side streets. They were the forgotten and obscure spots, the places that most of us, most likely, never visit.

That constant slimy rain was falling for days over the two cities. To better describe it, imagine the same drops you see on a normal rainy day with one small difference. Those drops did not consist of clear drops of water, but were dark purple, slimy matter. Now imagine those drops falling in a very specific order in very specific areas. Can you envision that?

Those were the invading aliens, being transported to the most obscure locations of our planet's surface, in the 1970 alien invasion that never happened. Does all this now ring a bell? Still, no memory whatsoever about this invasion?? Oh well.

Regardless, days went by and those falling drops started to accumulate, in a slow phase, into small dark purple and slimy hills.

The aliens' new transport method was taking shape and there was no one on Earth or in outer space that was able to stop it.

If you wanted to have a better understanding of the aliens' revolutionary transport method, you would have to grab a chair and spend a few hours in front of those hills, watching the falling drops and concentrating on their pattern. Only then could you appreciate the amazing accuracy of this complicated process. Most likely, it would make you wonder what other advanced technologies those aliens mastered. After all, this was the kind of technology humans could only dream about. Maybe then you could admire the ingenuity behind this invasion, which seemed to be orchestrated by very calculated and highly intellectual aliens. Oh yes!! They were an advanced nation that was able to transport and reassemble themselves out of dark purple, slimy drops – raindrops!

And I'll say it again. If you spent a few hours in front of those falling drops, you would achieve an enlightenment as never before, which would expend your horizons beyond your beliefs and change forever the way you think about life, creation, and even the universe.

But let's be realistic. Do you know anyone who has a few hours to spend just sitting and watching falling raindrops? Even if they are dark purple and slimy? I don't, and most likely you don't either. More than that, how many humans do you know that are actually capable of thinking about life, creation, and the universe at the same time?

There is no question that the aliens of the 1970 invasion were significantly more advanced than us and it wasn't hard to prove. Has it ever crossed your mind how much time we spent inventing something as simple as the wheel? Now try to remember how much additional time we had to spend, trying to figure out what to do with that wheel. That should give you a better idea of our achievements. And, please, don't get me started about what we went through developing indoor plumbing and flush toilets.

The drops came from up above, as far as the eye could see. Even if anyone tried to see, they wouldn't be able to trace their source, but since no one cared to look up, that source was never revealed. It's not that we were used to seeing dark purple, slimy drops falling on us. We just don't care for dark purple, slimy drops falling on us.

To be truthful, most humans don't care about lots of things that happen around them as long as they are not affected directly – not today and not in 1970.

It is very simple - city people just don't care for such events. You see, for city people anything that falls from up above is a daily occurrence. It might be a passing bird, relieving itself of an extra load, or a human, too impatient enough to wait for the elevator, taking the shortcut to the sidewalk. City people have much more important things to worry about. Since they are always pressed for time and on the run, they'll concentrate their attention only on those more important events in their lives, the ones that do affect them directly. Yes, I am talking about those events that can define our living standard such as: "Did you see our neighbor's new car?" "Do you know how much our neighbor's new car cost?" And most important: "Can we afford a better car than our neighbor's?"

The drops continued falling in formation, mounting slowly into small, slimy hills, and at the same time revealing the sad truth of this drop process. While the alien army's transformation to liquid matter at the point of origin was fast, their reassembly at the destination point was rather slow, very slow. The first to recognize this problem were the spaceships' pilots, who were in charge of their army's transportation to our planet's surface. They immediately contacted their scientists back home, starting their transmission with, "It is not our fault, but something is not right." They didn't want to take the blame for this excruciatingly sluggish process.

Only then were their scientists willing to admit that they had failed to mention this small issue. Unlike transporting a small frog over a short distance, transporting a full grown alien from outer space onto a planet surface could be much more complicated and maybe even slower, adding that since they had never tested it, they couldn't say for sure. However, they did say that any attempt to stop that process would result in the complete destruction of the aliens' army, the whole twenty thousand strong. Since the transport process was now deemed to last for weeks and with no alternative, it became an unexpected setback. In other words, in 1970 there was no one in our solar system who could stop that aliens' invasion that never happened, including the aliens themselves.

That news didn't sit well with the spaceships' pilots. Their scientists' new information just reaffirmed what they were worried about. They were about to be screwed again, just like their buddy the scouting mission pilot. They would be stuck parking in outer space for the long run with nothing to do. They were left with no other choice, but to find a constructive way to pass this extended and unexpected delay without abandoning their post. Finally, they resorted to playing a game, a very, very long game.

As time passed, the purple, slimy hills took the shape of what seemed to resemble a pair of thick, dark purple legs, which were just standing there in the small, back alleys behind the little mom & pop shops. The legs were toned and shaped like an alien Greek sculpture. They were colored in a shiny, glossy, dark purple skin speckled with a light purple, dotted pattern and were attached to dark wide, purple feet equipped with four manicured small toes each. To the best of my understanding, that was the exact moment in time that was entered into the aliens' historical records, when the great alien army set foot for the first time on Earth's surface, but since it was nothing more than the great alien army's feet, it was a very short historical entry.

Now the invading alien army consisted of no more than twenty thousand pairs of feet that couldn't go anywhere. They were just standing, waiting for additional drops to fall, moving forward slowly through the assembly process. Then came the aliens' knees, which were dark and purple, and days later, with the help of additional drops, the thighs and buttocks. All were covered with the same shiny, glossy, dark purple skin and the same light purple dotted pattern.

Can you imagine this sight? Half alien body, two legs and a rump, standing, hidden in our back alleys and small streets with nowhere to go and nothing to do.

How it can be that all the passing humans ignored a sight like that. Well, maybe they assumed that those aliens, in their current condition, were a part of a movie set or the work of a hipster artist. Remember that even today in the cities of Los Angeles and San Francisco, we have more than our fair share of movie sets and hipster artists. Maybe, as each alien began to take shape, they mistook them for damaged mannequins, left outside to be collected at the next trash pickup. Regardless, the grueling drop process was forging ahead and the alien army was going through the assembly process, with no deliberate interference what so ever from Earth's inhabitants.

It took an additional two weeks for this precise and delicate process to produce the aliens' thick torso, which had the same shiny, glossy, dark purple skin and the same light purple dotted pattern, but with one exception. Its lean and sculptured alien stomach was covered in a lighter, smoother, glossy shade of purple.

How can it be that our culture, with its tunnel vision, was so self-centered that it didn't notice these unfolding events? After all, there was a whole alien army, twenty thousand of them, reassembling right under our very noses, and we didn't notice a thing!! Well, thinking about it, since we do have tunnel vision and we are a self-absorbed society, it might just happen that anything that is below nose level can elude us, and go completely unnoticed. And since those aliens were only four and a half feet tall – it was very possible.

But to be truthful, this alleged invasion that never happened didn't go without a hitch or human interaction. On the contrary, from the get-go and throughout different stages of the assembly process there were humans who observed the aliens and maybe even paid attention to the drop process.

Understand this – the 1970 alien invasion didn't move forward completely unnoticed. Believe it or not, there were two groups in our society that actually saw the incoming aliens. Two groups of humans, who, unlike the rest of us, seemed to possess a higher awareness to their surroundings, two groups that might even pay attention.

OK, they didn't give it their complete and undivided attention, but only a small part of it, which wasn't enough to trigger an alarm and prevent the invasion. I am sure that you are curious to know who those two exceptional groups of humans were.

If you were to assume that those groups were the ones who inspect and question our universe on daily basis, our NASA scientists and amateur astronomers, you'd be completely wrong.

As strange as it sounds, they were the ones who missed this invasion altogether.

The very same people who dedicated their lives to study our solar system, the stars of our galaxy and the vast universe, missed the whole event. For reasons I can't understand, they committed themselves to constantly search out beyond the skies with the hope of finding and maybe introducing a new life form to the rest of the human race. It seems that they were firm believers that we had a need for new friends.

All I can say is that, of all years, 1970 wasn't the year in which we wanted, whatsoever, to make new friends. Case in point: In 1970, we made sure to keep our soldiers and their guns all the way across the ocean, in Vietnam, stating to the rest of the world, especially to the people of Vietnam, that we were not looking to make new friends on Earth – period. With a bold statement like that, do you really think that we wanted to find friends from another planet?

Our NASA scientists and amateur astronomers were the brightest of us all. They were the bookworms, able to calculate any known floating object's movement in the vastness of outer space. They worked hard, searching for any life form's existence in our celestial neighborhood, but never found a thing. Now, when they had a chance to validate their life work, they missed it all. They never knew about the invasion that never happened, and they still don't know.

Simply said, they were too consumed in their lifelong search for aliens, that when it happened, they were too blind-sided to see it. Never leaving their observation decks, standing with their eyes glued to their giant telescope lenses, sitting in their parents' basements with our galaxy's charts, they over scrutinized the universe. In their relentless quest, they were transmitting a continuous pattern of weird sounds to outer space, hoping for a response from any life form who was kind enough to respond.

Ironically, the brightest among us underestimated every other life forms in our universe, assuming they would appreciate this continuous pattern of weird sounds over a simple "Hello" in plain English. To their knowledge, this continuously transmitted pattern translated into "hello and welcome" or at least that's what they were told in a "Star Trek" convention by a "Trekkie," alleging to be expert in the Klingon language. Instead, they were transmitting to outer space a continuous string of obscenities of such a vulgar nature, which in return produced the opposite result. It kept all aliens who intercepted it as far away as possible from our planet and the repulsive life forms that occupied it.

The only good thing that happened to the NASA scientists and the amateur astronomers was their complete lack of awareness of this invasion that never happened. Since we all know that *"what you don't know, can't hurt you,"* maybe it would be a good idea to keep this tale between us. Let's protect our elderly NASA scientists and amateur astronomers during their golden years and let's maintain their happy spirits in their retirement years. I guess what I'm asking is that we keep this story under wraps.

But that begs the question. If it wasn't the NASA scientists and amateur astronomers, then who the hell were the two groups who had firsthand experience with the arriving aliens? Who were the brave souls that stood on the front line of this invasion and, sadly, didn't move a finger to stop it?

Well, all I can tell you is that they weren't your typical local heroes. Since they were so clueless about their doings at the time of the invasion, there is also a slim chance they'll ever come forward to claim their fame. And this should come as no surprise, as they were not from the top echelon of our society. They could be rich or poor, black or white, tall or short or even smart or dumb – they were just humans, the kind you meet on a daily bases. But we can still distinguish between them and divide them into two very specific groups of humans, interesting groups to say the least.

The first group was made out of our cigarette smokers, the same ones who had that endless craving for the satisfying puff of a cigarette. The ones who enjoyed taking their cigarette breaks in the seclusion of the back alleys of their work place … the same dark alleys that were chosen by the aliens for their arrival. The smokers who were sitting on their makeshift seats, could not have had a better view of the incoming aliens. One might say that the falling purple drops were gathering into small purple hills, practically, in front of their faces, but nothing clicked.

How could they ignore a whole invading alien army materializing right in front of them? There is no way for them to miss the strange phenomenon, but apparently there was. It happened and explaining it will be very disturbing.

You see, this guys were blessed with a very limited attention span, which resulted in their inability to process more than a single thought at a time. Combine it with their short smoke breaks and there you go – they simply had no time to deal with the incoming aliens. They were spending so much time in arranging their makeshift seats just to have the pleasure of few puffs and then, as they were about to catch a glimpse of the falling drops, it happened. It was an annoyance of such proportion that it overtook them, eliminating any hope of becoming aware of the falling drops and the invading aliens.

What can be so pressing? What can be more important than an alien invasion in progress? What was so disturbing that they completely ignored the falling drops? Well, it was their cigarette lighters.

Those cheap, plastic lighters that you get for free in any convenience store were the reason for this distraction. They simply would not light!!

Now, for non-smokers it's a non-issue, but for cigarette smokers, it can make the difference between a good or bad smoke break. In all fairness it might even ruin the rest of their day. For a cigarette smoker, an underperforming cigarette lighter can mark the point where everything starts going downhill.

The cigarette smokers were twirling the lighter' wheel with their right thumb – no success; twirling it with their left thumb … no success. They were shaking it, tapping it, knocking it against the sidewalk – still, no success. And as their short break was quickly ending, this failing lighter issue was becoming more pressing. The smokers found themselves spending the majority of their short breaks dealing with their lighters and by doing so completely ignored the falling drops. Those faulty lighters made them frustrated, throwing their hands in the air, cursing and swearing. They were vowing that on their next trip to the convenience store they would acquire a better quality lighter. They would even spend a dollar or two and not compromise for the cheap lighter again – even if they got it for free.

Did it ever cross your mind how upset cigarette smokers calm themselves? Well, it is done mainly by them lighting another cigarette. Now, since the failed lighter already made them upset, they were trying to light another cigarette, only to get caught in that vicious cycle of the cheap and defective cigarette lighter. Their inability to light another cigarette only made them more upset and the vicious cycle continued.

Now you can see how it's possible for those cigarette smokers to completely ignore the forming aliens, right in front of their faces? As I've told you before, there was a simple and disturbing explanation. The cigarette smokers simply had no time for the incoming aliens.

Since there is nothing else I can add about the cigarette smokers, it would be a good time to introduce you to the second group of humans.

Now, this is the more interesting group of humans. At face value, we should give them some respect and maybe even consider them heroes. After all, they were the game changers that in a strange way diverted this invasion that never happened off its course. Somehow, they were able to cross paths with the invading aliens and in a very untraditional way, interact with them. Were those humans so brave that they were willing to stick their necks out for us? Well, it wasn't exactly like that.

It really was is that for no apparent reason, those humans just happened to be in the right place at the right time. They made a step forward and disrupted the alien invasion, and I do mean that they, literally, made one step forward and by that saved the human race. It is fair to say that they didn't plan to disrupt anything and, as a matter of fact, were never aware of their doings. After all, what does it take to put one foot in front of the other – not much. But if you do so and at the same time change the course of the 1970 aliens' invasion – that counts for a lot.

I know it sounds confusing, but let me clarify. You see, this group was made from the less fortunate in our society, the absent-minded among us or what we usually call the goofballs. Those are the ones who on a consistent basis step into trouble or adventure without their knowledge. Fortunately for them, in most cases, they will also step out of those situations without their knowledge. This invasion that never happened was one of those cases. They were, completely, oblivious to what they were stepping into or more accurately, what they stepped on. The fact was that they stepped into this invasion, right on top of the incoming aliens and they didn't do so on purpose.

They were on their way to work or enjoying a stroll on a beautiful, sunny California day, just minding their own business. Being absent-minded, they were daydreaming, allowing a smile to form in the corner of their mouths and then, completely unintentionally, it happened. Somehow, they managed to either walk right on top one of those dark purple, slimy hills or walk through the falling dark purple, slimy drops.

Either way their actions delivered catastrophic results to the aliens, reflecting in either the complete obliteration of some of the mounting hills or the disruption of the 10,473 drops, the exact number of drops required for an alien's complete reassembly. Those disrupted drops didn't reach their destination, but landed on those courageous humans' clothing. Those humans' actions resulted in the immediate annihilation of some aliens, ending their lives and reducing this invasion's chances of success.

Did our heroes celebrate their success? No, they didn't. Since they were counting their misfortune and not realizing their success, their initial response wasn't intelligent or impressive. Would you expect anything else from our absent-minded friends?

It came out as an outpouring string of obscenities, too graphic to put into writing. And they were rightly upset as all of their plans for that day had to be put on the backburner. Don't forget that the only thing they had left was a big mess on their hands. Well, if we would like to be more accurate, that same big mess was also on their shoes and on their clothing.

A few minutes later, they came to their senses, what I call the acceptance stage, and begin scanning their surroundings, looking in all directions, moving directly into what I call the realization stage. And no, they didn't look for the source of their misery, which most likely would reveal the incoming aliens. What they were looking for was for the fastest way to get rid of this messy, slimy, dark purple "stuff" that was stuck to their shoes and clothing.

Those who stepped on top of the dark purple hills were easy to trace around the small streets sidewalk curbs. They were doing their best to wipe the soles of their shoes against those curbs in an attempt to remove the slimy material. But those with the slimy stains on their clothing had a greater task on their hands as they were trying to find a prompt solution to those stains. They were in panic mode, making a mad dash through the cities' streets in a search for the closest dry-cleaning establishment. In their current condition only an immediate and decisive action, such as a deep stain removal, would result in success and maybe even save those articles of clothing.

Are you wondering why I consider these humans as heroes? Well, it's simple. You see, unlike the cigarette smokers who did nothing, our goofballs and their actions created major damage and chaos within the invading army's ranks. Without their knowledge, they put the aliens' well-organized invasion machine into complete disarray and it was all the result of a single absent-minded step they made. This small step altered the invasion's direction and ultimately dashed the aliens' aspirations to take over our planet. Now, how can you not consider these guys as our saviors?

Years later, the aliens established a committee to investigate the whereabouts of those missing aliens from the 1970 invasion of Earth. Their disappearance was a mystery no one could explain. At the end of this investigation, the committee had no clue about the reasons for their disappearance, but it allowed them to reveal publicly the extent of the damage and confusion their disappearance created. The committee also released an exact accounting of the missing aliens, including their names and ranks. Since the committee had no knowledge of our absent-minded humans' actions, they decided to categorize the lost aliens as missing in action (MIA) and their only recommendation was to honor the missing with a national memorial day, something the aliens never celebrated before, and to erect a new monument in their home planet's main square. This monument listed the missing aliens' names and ranks, which were etched onto one of its sides. And to say the least, it was a very impressive list.

It seems that our heroes inflicted major damage to the alien army. Among the names listed and between the hundreds of foot soldiers who disappeared without a trace, you could also trace the names of aliens of the highest ranks and above. It seems that somehow the absent-minded humans managed to walk through and eliminate this invasion's chief architects, the two top generals who were responsible for the invasion's effective execution. They also managed to wipe out the invasion's four communication officers, who were critical for this invasion's success. They were the ones who were assigned the task of transmitting the "All Clear" signal to the large spaceships in outer space, initiating the second stage of the invasion, the delivery of supplies and weapons to the ground forces. The remains of those officers were scraped off our absent-minded humans' shoes on the curbs of the same back streets, where the officers had initially dropped.

But if we compare the fate of the two top generals and four communication officers to the fate of the entire aliens' translation team, the generals and communication officers had it easy. Their end was fast and swift.

The aliens' translation team was made of highly intelligent aliens who had invested the last years of their lives in studying and perfecting their knowledge of the humans' language. Their assignment was to engage and interact with Earth's population while securing the initial parking spaces in Walmart's huge parking lots and at the same time preventing misconceptions about unarmed, purple invading aliens.

Unfortunately for those poor bastards, their demise was cruel beyond imagination. They, or more accurately, parts of them, in the form of slimy purple drops, stained our goofballs' clothing and ended in the belly of industrial dry-cleaning machines of the latest model. They were aggressively removed like common dirt from some T-shirts and executives' suit jackets. To the best of my knowledge, their last resting place was "Mr. Chang's One Day Dry Cleaning," which in 1970 was the closest dry-cleaning store to the same small back allies were they arrived.

And to make their last moments even more unsettling, Mr. Chang insisted on processing those stained clothing twice through his industrial dry-cleaning machine of the latest model with a generous amount of added bleach. Mr. Chang argued that it was the sure and only way to achieve the best results. Mr. Chang also made sure to charge accordingly, double the regular price, but he was generous enough not to charge for the added bleach.

May the poor souls of the aliens' entire translation team rest in peace at the bottom of this industrial dry-cleaning machine of the latest model.

And our goofballs never knew a thing…

While those events were transpiring, the rest of the alien army continued reassembling, completely in the dark. Since that army was already very frustrated from the snail-paced drop process, maybe it was for the best. I am sure that the knowledge of this devastation all around them wouldn't help a bit.

Nevertheless, the remaining drops continued coming at a slow and monotonous pace. That slow process scared away even the few humans who might have had an infinitesimal interest in this once in a lifetime, unexplained event. It was such a slow process that seemed as if it was going nowhere and as a result drove everyone away. And that was understandable.

After all it is a known fact that we, humans, only care about things we can make sense of. Dark, purple, slimy drops collected at such a slow pace and with no end in sight, definitely do not fit into this category. Those are the type of events we really don't care about or notice should you even dangle them right in front of our faces. And that explains why we missed the creation of the aliens' arms and hands, which were covered with the same pattern and equipped with a pair of medium size, manicured, sharp claws for fingers.

At first glance those claws were nasty and scary looking, but a second inspection revealed they weren't good for a lot. What can any double clawed animal or creature, including an intelligent alien, do in our world? Not much!! At most it can hold a napkin or at best a towel. There is no way for him to handle any device that wasn't developed specifically for his claws. What I am trying to say is that other than those weird shaped ray guns developed especially for their use on their planet; those guys had no chance handling any kind of weapon, especially human weapons. Since the aliens came with no weapons of their own, there lay a new issue. It seems that those claws were useless, but then came a new revelation.

It seems there was one thing those claws could do and did pretty well, a by-product that appeared at the time of their creation, an interesting feature made of an ongoing clicking sound that resembled our finger snapping, which in 1970 considered to be a cool activity. Since, it is a matter of opinion to say what is cool and what is not, all I can say is that clicking sound was cool in 1970 and is not that cool today.

Now, you could hear that sound coming from every corner where the aliens were assembling. It was an ongoing "click, click, click, click" sound, but this time it wasn't a mishap. It wasn't another failure in the aliens' slow transportation process, but an intended act of the materializing aliens. You see, the very frustrated semi-assembled aliens who had been standing for days headless and incapable of movement, resorted to the one thing they could do - claw snapping. They were upset and wanted to protest, but since they were headless, they literally had no mouth to voice their grievances or complain to one another. So, the impatient aliens resorted to the one thing they were able to do, clicking their claws nonstop as an outlet for their frustration. It was the only logical reaction they could come up with. They weren't happy at all, but they were full of hope.

And what they were hoping for? They were hoping that upon their return to their home planet, they would get together with the same scientists who had developed this damn drop process in the most remote area of the most remote docking space of their planet. They were hoping to have five minutes alone with those scientists, believing that it was a sufficient amount of time for them to personally thank those S.O.B's for that brilliant process they developed. They were hoping that their supervisor would allow them to open one of those sealed air locks and release those idiot scientists into the vacuum of outer space.

In 1970, that clicking and snapping sounded exactly as the snapping sound from that famous scene of the popular movie "West Side Story" in which a white gang, dressed with their tight pants, are snapping their fingers while doing their manly dance alone the city back allies on their way to confront the Puerto Rican gang, with their tight pants and manly dance.

For our young readers, this movie released in 1961, long before you were born, and made when dancing routines of men in tight pants who snap their fingers was a cool thing.

Cool or not, that clicking sound removed the element of surprise, which the aliens cared so much about, and reached the humans. We heard that sound coming from the back alleys, but had no grasp of its source or the danger that came with it. The only thing we knew was that it sounded like "West Side Story" and that we had to act accordingly. So what did we do? We did the first thing that came to our minds and it wasn't questioning that sound's source, investigating its origin or even eliminating it. What did we do? We danced!

And was there any better place to dance then in the back alleys of Los Angeles and San Francisco? Flash dance mobs would just pop up, spontaneously, and dance through those back alleys while snapping their fingers to the clicking rhythm, replicating the movie's dancing scene. They would dance their way down the street and disappear in the same spontaneous way they appeared.

When asked, the dancers admitted that hearing this clicking sound gave them an unexplained urge to dance. After all, we all know that a real dancer will always have an unexplained urge to dance to any background noise, even to the sound of his own kitchen dishes, shattered by his upset wife during a heated argument.

Additional time passed and the drop process was about to be completed and with it came the creation of the aliens' heads, at least the heads of the remaining aliens. There were maybe an additional thirty to forty drops to go for full completion, but by now you could see the long process's final product. The aliens were equipped with a large head in the shape of an upside down triangle, proportionally bigger than the rest of their bodies. It had the same dark purple color and the same light, shiny purple dotted pattern. It was populated with two pointy ears, two large round white eyes with blue and black metallic eyeballs, wide purple nose and a large mouth equipped with a bunch of little sharp teeth.

A large mouth with a bunch of little sharp teeth? It must have been the focal point of the aliens' faces and, by all accounts, it meant to be scary and intimidating. Well, not exactly – here is where the monkey wrench came into play. Unfortunately for the aliens, it wasn't scary at all. You see, it was then, when the aliens realized that our planet was a bigger joker than them and had just pulled its own cruel joke.

What happened was that our planet's gravity had made its own contribution to the reassembled aliens and it was all over their faces, specifically on that large mouth with the bunch of little sharp teeth.

Earth's gravity, quite simply, changed the mouth's natural shape, raising its two corners, creating everlasting grins. The aliens' mouths, which were famous across the universe for its upset demeanor, were now stamped with a constant smile. The aliens had a persistent smirk on their faces. To put it in layman's terms, they were not scary anymore.

In their wildest dreams and during this invasion planning, could the aliens envision such a setback and the only thing they could do was to add it to their never-ending and always growing list of setbacks. Throughout history there had never been an invasion, by humans or aliens, in which the invading forces were equipped with an everlasting smirk on their faces, while attempting to take over a planet or even a small country. How can anyone install fear or authority over a conquered nation when all he can offer is a smile with a bunch of white teeth and a cheerful personality? Needless to say, the aliens were not happy about this unexpected detour, but still couldn't stop smiling.

The process was almost done and there stood the aliens: Four and a half feet tall with dark purple skin and a shiny, light purple dotted pattern all over their bodies; a fairly large face that was crowned with a larger smiling mouth full of teeth. Oh that smile…

I am sure of the invading aliens' awareness of this mishap, but not so sure if they understood its consequences.

All together they were just funny-looking, borderline cute creatures who were still clicking that "West Side Story" snapping sound with their manicured claws as they were waiting for the last fifteen drops. That's all they needed, the last fifteen drops that would bring the drop total to the required 10,473 drops and, for the love of god, end that damn process. They were standing in their spots, unhappy and frustrated, but to their credit I must say that putting their feelings aside, they never stopped smiling.

What would you do if a creature with the same general description approached you? How would you react if it insisted that your planet had been invaded by him and his buddies and that you must comply with his demands? How seriously would you take this creature when you saw that huge smile on his face? And how long would you be able to keep a straight face before you start laughing your ass off? In other words, after all I've told you, is there any chance that you could consider this invasion that never happened as a serious invasion?

Finally the drop process ended. If we forget the ginormous time delay and ignore our aliens' smiling faces, we can say that up to this point the invasion was moving forward as planned. Somehow the aliens succeeded to cross galaxies, reach our planet, and land in our back yard unnoticed.

The same goes with their pilots who were able to stay occupied on the large spaceships in outer space and hadn't left their post and abandoned their army. The aliens were slowly gathering into groups in the small back alleys. They were so thrilled to see their friends. Their mood became better as they were greeting each other, saying hello and shaking claws while stretching their muscles, releasing leg cramps from their long standing in one place. They were pumped and ready, waiting for instructions. They had stood for too long and were ready to start the next step in this invasion that never happened, expecting the "Go Ahead" command from their generals, authorizing them to get out from those back alleys and take over the cities' main streets and its human population. Simply put, the aliens' army was waiting for the command to INVADE!!!

As you might already guess, that order never came. It never came since at that specific moment, the invasion's top two generals were nothing but a dark purple, thick and slimy mess stuck to the bottom of some unlucky, absent-minded humans' shoes. Let's just say that the generals were not in any position to give orders. A short time after, as the alien army realized that nothing is happening; they started losing their composure, realizing that something had gone wrong and their generals were nowhere to be found. The absence of their four communication officers didn't go unnoticed as well. It made the situation even worse. It dawned on the aliens they were stuck on Earth's surface, unable to communicate with their pilots, unable to request support, supplies, directions or even, at bare minimum, new communication officers.

While they were counting their losses, to add insult to injury, the aliens couldn't trace the whereabouts of their entire translation team. That was a catastrophic revelation, which in their eyes was even worse than the loss of their generals and communication officers. Without the translation team members, the aliens would be completely misunderstood on our planet. That forced them into a new reality in which they become aliens on our planet ... and this time for real.

In this new reality, the aliens were stripped of everything they had, and left standing in the back alleys, lost and confused with no direction, supplies or support. The only thing they were left with was their complete lack of communication with the local population... us.

The alien army was in a bad spot, stuck on our planet with nothing. They didn't even have the sufficient funds to purchase one of those pre-made sandwiches in our convenience stores, something that doesn't sound as such a big deal, but for any military person is a very big deal. You see, the alien army wasn't any different than any other army, including our own. Like any other army they were brought up to believe that an army cannot fight on an empty stomach. Since they had nothing to eat for days, their stomachs were empty and there was no point in starting a fight.

To the few passing humans they looked quite miserable. You see, the humans mistook the aliens for those who lived in the shadows of our society. For them it was a sad spectacle, thinking of the aliens as their fellow human being in distress. Acting out of mercy, they handed the aliens spare change and used articles of clothing, assuming they were helping someone in need.

For now, the aliens would not step into our cities' main streets, but remained in the comfort of the secluded back alleys and waited, hoping that it was only a matter of time before they would receive a whole new command structure, new generals, communication officers and an entirely new translation team. For now, they would live on humans' handouts, which they had learned to enjoy. They loved everything the humans gave them. Most of all, like the 1967 scouts, they became infatuated with the sixties' clothing and it was just a matter of time before the whole alien army found itself covered in colorful sixties garments.

It started to look as if the aliens didn't want to abandon the security of the back alleys. By then, they were all dressed up, killing time and waiting for the right moment to make their move.

After a long waiting, they realized no help would come from above and were left with no other choice, but to give up the coziness of those alleys and step into our main streets.

Those aliens were from a highly intelligent specie, definitely more intelligent than us. Did you ever see humans materialize from a bunch of collected drops? Those funny looking, short, purple, smiling aliens were capable of controlling and executing an extremely accurate and delicate process. Can you imagine the mechanics behind such technology? To control the elements of nature and gravity there were two essential qualities one must possess, trust and patience. It seems the aliens had a hold of those qualities and were able to execute them simultaneity. This is something humans cannot do. It is true, most of us do not possess trust or patient and even the few among us who do, can't execute those qualities at the same time.

How can you reach higher levels if you can't trust the one how push you? How can you build and reach new heights if you are impatient with your peers? Raise these questions with our aliens and hopefully you'll understand their answer. After all, they were able to put those to qualities to work with great success. They were able to reach new heights and from there, it was a cakewalk for them to innovate such technologies we can only dream of, including this delicate and highly questionable drop process.

Since we established that humans cannot materialize from drops, it would be fair to say that humans will consider this idea crazy and impossible. Even today, with all of our advancements in the technology and medical fields, we still can't imagine such process. That might be the reason, why most of you will smile and dismiss my tale about aliens who invaded California in 1970 as purple rain drops for the sole purpose of finding replacement "Double AA" batteries for an old cassette player so they could listen to Jimi Hendrix's music…

How do I know this, you ask? Well, it is from my personal experience.

You see, the few who I've told about the aliens' invasion that never happened were unable to keep a straight face as they were trying to determine if I'd lost it completely or was just being funny. It goes without saying that since then most of them do their best to avoid me. Maybe, like them, you are wondering how I can be so sure about this invasion that never happened? Well, I'm not surprised, the same way I'm not surprised that no one else remembers this invasion. It is a classic "Catch 22" scenario. You must be crazy to believe that an invasion like that did happen while at the same time invading a planet as purple rain drops just to obtain replacement "Double AA" batteries is a crazy idea. Simply said, how can anyone believe this invasion really happened if it was a crazy idea to begin with?

It wouldn't be easy for me to convince you that this invasion that never happened, really happened. The invading aliens left no trace behind. Even if they had left a sign, such as their famous huge crop circles, most of you would dismiss it, calling it a marketing stunt by a lawnmower company.

Regardless, there is one thing I know for sure and it is that in 1970, in the back alleys of the small streets of Los Angeles and San Francisco, there was a whole alien invasion force, twenty thousand strong. They were much smarter and technologically advanced than us. They had just finished getting reassembled as their almost perfect invasion of our planet was at its height. And after a long wait they had gained their composure and were in the process of regrouping and creating structure within their ranks.

The aliens, who finally realized they were on their own, decided to take charge of their own destiny. They were ready to execute the invasion that never happened.

Chapter 8 – The Invasion That Never Happened

Another memorable moment, a new entry in their historical record, began when the aliens initiated their invasion's second stage, and stepped out from the safety of the back alleys onto the bright and dangerous main streets of the two cities.

The historical record described how they came out in small, semi-organized groups. It also marked that moment as the first time were the invading forces had the pleasure of encountering California's general population, which didn't exactly meet their expectations.

Having no command and control structure, the aliens had only a general idea of what they were supposed to do and how to do it. To the best of their knowledge, they had to take over humanity and assume control over a large stock of replacement "Double AA" batteries at the same time. Those were their general goals when they stepped into our streets, but unfortunately for them, things didn't transpire as they hoped.

And no wonder. You see, here on Earth we have this ancient rule, which was around humanity since the beginning of time. This rule is simple and disturbing at the same time as it clearly states that *"Anything that can go wrong – will go wrong."* After so many centuries of dealing with this cruel rule, humans stopped complaining about it and accepted it at face value. In 1949 we even gave it a name: "Murphy's Law." The aliens, on the other hand, never heard of this rule and never named it, maybe because they never had the pleasure of experiencing it or meeting Murphy. Now as they were starting to interact with us, they earned the opportunity to meet this rule, front and center, and maybe even eventually give it a name of their own.

You see, it is one thing to stand in the dark back allies and prepare for the execution of some general goals, but it is a different ball game to move forward to attain those goals when your appearance is so cute and funny. It was something they didn't anticipate, to appear so adorable, short and colored in two shades of shiny purple with a large face and even a larger smile. But if that wasn't enough to sabotage their plans, they had no weapons.

How can anyone consider invading a planet without weapons? Ask the 1970 alien invasion forces that same question and they will do their best to convince you it was doable. Just let them talk for a few minutes and see how, eventually, they would come around and agree that their explanation sounds dumb and embarrassing.

In their original invasion plans, which included two high ranking generals, four accomplished communication officers, and the English language experts of the entire translation team, the aliens had every reason to leave their weapons behind, and that includes their spacecraft with the big ray guns and their personal side arms. After all, they knew that a single short transmission to their pilots would initiate the immediate delivery of all of that equipment.

In their minds it was simple, a single short transmission was all that was required. Never, in their wildest dreams, could they imagine there would be no communication officers to initiate this very short yet very critical transmission. Now, as the new reality was settling in on the stranded aliens, they understood that the chance of them contacting their war machines in outer space was slim. After all this waiting and since they hadn't see anything transpire in the skies above them, it dawned on them that they were alone, stuck on our planet unable to receive their supplies and weapons. Unfortunately for them - they were correct.

You see, during the excruciatingly slow drop process, their pilots became bored with the long wait and looked for an activity that would alleviate their boredom. When the process finished, the pilots were in the midst of an alien game called *"I spy with my little metallic eye."* They were using our "Milky Way" galaxy and its three hundred billion stars as their board game, challenging each other to trace and name each of those stars, and I do mean each of the three hundred billion stars. The more they got into the game, the less they paid attention to the drop process monitors. Let's just say it wasn't long before the pilots completely forgot about their army on Earth's surface. That was the last straw, which convinced the stranded alien army to engage our society empty-handed.

It wasn't an act of bravery, but of over-confidence. As much as they were concerned about their missing side arms, the aliens were still very confident they could still attain success, at least for the short run. What made them so confident, you ask? Why would they believe we would submit to their demands? Again, the way they saw it – there was a simple answer.

You see, across the vast universe those aliens were known as its "Hell's Angels." They would Ride their modified, fully loaded, shiny spaceships at high speed across galaxies, from one horizon to another, always making sure to make enough noise to intimidate anyone in their surroundings. There was an unspoken understanding between them and the universe's occupants, in which it was in your best interest to keep your distance from them. Should you ride any of the universe's highways and see sparkling bright lights moving very fast toward you, slowly transforming into a fully loaded shiny spaceship, it was in your best interest to move aside, park, and give the right of way to those space bad boys.

It continued suggesting that it wouldn't be a bad idea for you to pray to your alien gods, begging that those aliens wouldn't stop for a "chat." Should you be out-of-luck or maybe just ignored by your gods and they did stop for a chat, try to contact your alien gods one last time, asking them to keep those thugs in good mood. After all, no one wants to have to call a spaceship towing service for his floating beyond repair, trashed vessel.

This unspoken understanding, this universal fact was the reason for our invading aliens' over-confidence. In their minds, they had the upper hand in their quest to conquer our society. Unfortunately for them, there was this small little detail, they didn't consider, a tiny problem. You see, while this unspoken understanding was widely known across the vast universe, it never reached planet Earth or the self-centered society that occupied it. We never heard about the "Hell's Angels" of our universe.

So, to their astonishment, they were completely ignored by Earth's inhabitants. Come on, we were really busy. In 1970 we had so many things on our plates, not to mention the Vietnam War, and had no time for adorable, smiling aliens. We were trying to remain vocal and opinionated, trying to move forward. Everyone did their best to be heard, making everyone else aware of their existence. There were rallies, marches, demonstrations, and parties to keep us occupied and we were not paying attention to the short, purple creatures, who at no point made us feel they were a threat from outer space.

Yes, they were walking among us, but we ignored them. There were some humans who gave the aliens a glance and, mistakenly, assumed them to be a walking, talking toy released by one of the major toy companies. They would walk away wondering where they could purchase such adorable puppets? And if it was safe to buy a toy equipped with sharp, manicured claws? Most of all they were trying to figure out how hard it would be to wrap such a toy without tearing the wrapping paper to shreds!

In contrast to most of us, there were some humans who didn't disregard the aliens. These were the Black Panthers and the Hippies who met the alien scouts three years earlier. Since the aliens were all lookalike, they believed those aliens were their long lost friends who had disappeared three years before with no explanation or forwarding address. When they encountered them they took immediate action. Without hesitation, they grabbed the aliens by the arm and dragged them to the nearest demonstration, recruiting them back to their lines.

Once again, the members of the Black Panthers and Hippies movements accepted the aliens with open arms, no questions asked. Be that as it may, the last three years had changed them. It was the sign of the times. 1970 was definitely different than 1967, which was reflected in the members of the two movements who were more intense. Without a word, they gave the aliens large signs and positioned them right in front of the nightly television crews' cameras. The aliens' reappearance was heaven-sent for them. They were holding those large signs for too many years. They were tired and in desperate need of a fresh pair of hands, even if they were a substandard pair of claws.

I went through as many hours of that old newsreel footage I could put my hands on, looking for proof that this invasion that never happened, did happen, attempting to trace the aliens' faces in the crowd. It seems that, for one reason or another, in all of that footage the aliens' faces got obstructed by the large signs they were holding. The only thing you can see is something that resembled a pair of very long, beautifully manicured nails holding those large signs' corners. Since very long, beautifully manicured nails were "En Vogue" in 1970 women's fashion, it is impossible to prove who those manicured nails belonged to, the aliens or the ladies of 1970.

These aliens never met the Black Panthers or the Hippies before. They didn't understand why those pushy humans dragging them all across the cities, by their arms. But still they obliged. For them it was a matter of choice, either to be completely ignored or to accommodate the few humans that gave them the time of day. Their initial encounter with us wasn't encouraging as it crushed that over confidence they had and replaced it with insecurities. It was the last thing they expected after the tedious training they went through in preparation for this invasion, another detour. Why would the humans be so inconsiderate? They couldn't put a finger on this. After all, what did they ask for? To take over our planet?

Do you know how disappointing it is for a highly intelligent aliens, authorities across the universe, to be dismissed so lightly by humans, a low-level and primitive society? Can you understand how discouraging it was for them to realize that they are not just being ignored by the humans, but also by their own pilots? For them it was an enigma. What have they done to their pilots to be treated like that? They just realized that conquering Earth and taking over its population wasn't going to be an easy task. It was another crack in their plans, which marked the beginning of the end of the invasion that never happened.

But I'm getting ahead of myself. It was too early for them to quit. They didn't go through it all just to throw in the towel. Instead, they will use everything at their disposal to get our attention. That included jumping into the path of passing humans in an attempt to distract them, resorting to hand gestures and intimidating facial expressions. In some rare cases they even gripped a human's leg and were dragged for at least a few blocks.

The aliens were tailing and stalking the rushing humans, trying to follow them wherever they went, turning it into a game of catch up. And what was the end game? Well, at this point it wasn't any more about taking over our planet. It was about something much more basic - recognition. They wanted us to acknowledge them, to reaffirm their existence among us.

And so it happened that in 1970, on the main streets of Los Angeles and San Francisco, you could trace purple, short aliens shadowing humans, walking their funny walk, flapping their purple arms in the air and making the same familiar clicking sound with their claws. They were waiting for humans in the large parking lots, following them into the huge shopping malls, something that didn't work that well. It was those shopping malls' large revolving doors that would become their pitfall, trapping them each and every time. It was easy to trace one or more aliens stuck in those revolving doors, spinning round and round, trying to figure a way out from this ultimate, human deathtrap.

If luck was on their side, it wouldn't be long before one of our absent-minded humans, the same goofballs who brought some aliens to an early grave, would show up and commit the same blunder, getting trapped as well. For this goofball, it would only be a matter of time to collect his thoughts and find his way out - that's when the aliens would follow him quickly, escaping into the mall's large interior, hyperventilating and recuperating from that stressful imprisonment. Now they had a new problem on their hands, figuring a way out while being careful not to step into another vicious, human trap, the mall escalators.

In one of their attempts to establish their authority over us, they moved into threat mode, comprised of the most dramatic and chilling quotes from their alien literature. But since they were using their native tongue, we didn't understand a word and all those threats fell on deaf ears.

Still hoping for a miracle and since nothing else worked in their favor, the aliens resorted to another attempt to get our attention. They moved to recite a monologue they wrote in a very short time, hoping that we grasp some bits and pieces. But since they were still using their native tongue, this recital also fell on deaf ears.

Everyone could hear them, but no one listened. Why would we care to understand this discordant, high-pitched sound, which we considered white noise - gibberish?

Now, after all those years, I can tell you what their monologue was all about. It was a simple and polite request for us to surrender. They were asking, if it was at all possible, for us to submit and raise our hands in a gesture of good faith. The way they saw it, submission was an important component in the behavior of any normal invaded society and it wasn't just their opinion, but the opinion of any other alien society they encountered in the universe.

They were correct, that was the way of every other normal society across the universe. But what they failed to understand was that, this time, they weren't dealing with a normal society.

And we are not a normal society, even though we claim to be. We tend to believe that no one else is as normal as us and that it is our first and foremost duty to educate everyone to be like us, you know - normal. Case in point, in 1970, we were spending so much energy, convincing everyone else to adopt our set of beliefs that we completely ignored a full-scale alien invasion that happened right under our noses.

The aliens did their best, using any means to invade planet Earth, but with no direction, reinforcements, supplies or communication, always found themselves on the short end of the stick. That led to another change in their tactics. Since the humans would not submit to their demands, the aliens would change their tone one last time and use the only weapon at their disposal – begging.

They had no choice, their name was on the line. They hadn't made this long journey from a faraway galaxy and gone through this frustrating "Drop Process" just to be rejected. They wanted us to understand this, to know that they didn't come in peace, and that any sign of their mission's failure would result in them becoming the laughingstocks of the universe.

But we didn't understand or care to listen, and that turned a hopeless situation into a ridiculous one. What is more pathetic than an alien chasing a human, trying to get recognition? Especially when it's using clicking claws and a signature smiling face to attract the human's undivided attention. Add to this the aliens' funny walk, and it turns a scary invading alien into what looks like a talented flamenco dancer. Now, how can anyone get upset with a talented flamenco dancer?

Humans can. It wasn't just because 1970's Californians didn't care for foreign, flamenco dancers with a poor knowledge of the English language, but also because we've developed an interesting way to handle ourselves with foreigners, in that we simply close our eyes and ignore aliens in need. One might say there is nothing wrong with that. After all, we are a society that cannot accommodate changes which come without advanced notice, including listening and understanding a foreign language. The listening part is the one that makes it so hard.

Maybe we are a closed-minded society, but there is an upside to this. Can you imagine what we would have to do if we understood those foreign languages? Don't forget that foreigners can be very annoying and needy. They always come up with weird questions like, "Can you tell me where the bathroom is?" and "Is this the Statue of Liberty?" Helping an alien in need means altering our daily routine, which is unacceptable. Instead, we would rather change our daily routine, making sure not to cross paths with the ones in need and that includes crossing to the other side of the street. Let's be fair, we're not that good in helping foreigners, and until a foreigner finds his place in our society, he'll be in constant need of hand holding, something that can drive you batty.

In the following days and weeks, the aliens tried to pitch to us their invasion plans. It was something about what they believed to be a great opportunity for us to give up our way of life, our freedom and free spirit, letting them assume control of every aspect of our lives. It was about the aliens' belief that they were doing us a favor.

Suddenly, or maybe finally, something clicked with the aliens. It dawned on them that their timing was wrong. You see, the things they wanted us to give up were exactly the same things we were fighting to keep. There was no way we would give away our freedom, free spirit or way of life. We lived in a very special era and all around us there were new ideas and opportunities, and none of them mentioned submission to aliens.

The aliens were unable to take over our planet and they knew it. They were fighting a losing battle, and it all boiled down to the simple fact that they were unable to open a channel of communication with us. Maybe they even wanted to give up on this whole invasion, but they were in a bind. They couldn't figure out the source for the very much-needed replacement "Double AA" batteries.

Does this shed more light on how this invasion that supposedly happened, never happened? Can you understand how all of us completely missed this intergalactic conflict that practically landed in our laps? I don't know for certain the reasons this conflict was so invisible. Maybe it was the lack of firearms, explosions, and casualties on both sides. After all, those are the things that keep us interested and excited in any of our Earthly conflicts.

Examining the whole scenario from a human point of view, it would be easy for us to say that the aliens failed miserably in their attempt to invade our planet and not because they didn't leave their mark on every high-rise building or create a new chapter in our history. It wasn't also because we were never aware of their existence among us. They failed because they unable to invade our personal space. There is nothing more important to humans than their personal space – ask anyone.

We all know that there is a time and a place for everything. Any success story you've heard about, mostly happened in the right place and at the right time. It wasn't any different with the aliens' invasion, which without any question was done in a decent place. California of 1970 was the right place. The Golden State opened its doors to any visitor, allowing them to blend into its mix of cultures without any problems, aliens included. The time, on the other hand, was wrong. The aliens' attempt to invade California, USA in 1970 occurred at the wrong time, giving them zero chance for success.

Ask anyone who was there, in the late sixties and early seventies and they would all agree those were unique and different times. Well, 1970 was right smack in the middle of that time. Everyone became bolder, insisting on being heard, becoming more vocal and opinionated. All across the nation there was this outcry, a desperate need, for individuality and California residents were no different. They always tended to define their individuality, something that wasn't limited to their opinions or the car parked in their driveway.

But there was something else that throughout history allowed humans to define themselves in their quest for individuality. We used it to project our feelings and state of mind, and in 1970 as a way to protest. It played an important part in our human evolution and as time went by we gave it a name. We called it: Fashion!

If you ask, what can I tell you about that period's fashion? I would tell you that you should ask: what can't I tell you about it? It was special and reflected the sign of the times. It had personality and meaning, carrying an exceptional message for generations to come, woven into very colorful garments. You can easily recognize it in the period's social movements and their grand purpose. They used their apparel as a way to promote their cause and a way to establish their existence among us. As they were doing so and without their knowledge, they made an additional and very important contribution to our history.

This colorful generation who was lucky to live in such colorful times and stand on the world's main stage, made sure to leave its mark on history with very colorful garments, their very own fashion. It is true that they were written and remembered in history for their constant fight for social changes, but there is no way to overlook their fashion and the everlasting impression it left behind. Now, give me the opportunity to tell you a little more about their fashion.

You see, by 1970 we had something new in our lives – the ability to contest the existing status quo. We were able to develop our own way of life and be proud of our choices. We used fashion to reflect our personalities. Some of us chose to dress in the unmistakable and familiar Black Panthers' paramilitary clothing, which was a combination of a black leather jacket, white T-shirt, black pants, topped with a black beret. If you really wanted to show that you meant business, black shades were a must. Wearing the Black Panthers' clothing wasn't a joke, but a serious statement, defining your discontent with the status quo.

Wearing the Hippies' clothing, on the other hand, was a completely different story. It was a relaxed fashion statement of a relaxed state of mind, a loose fashion that held an infinite choice of clothing, easy to create from any combination of garments in your closet, but one that still required some common sense and healthy imagination. After all, no one wanted to walk the streets mistaken for a clown. Those who wore this fashion weren't any different from their Black Panther counterparts. Their message was different, of love and peace and they chose to reflect it in the colors of the rainbow. But they had a strong message in mind and wanted to be heard.

Since the beginning of time, fashion had been an important component in our lives, but at every given time it came with a daily challenge. How many times have you found yourself standing, staring at your clothing, wondering what to wear? We were looking for an answer to this question, for an easy way out, and somewhere in our history, we found the solution. We started imitating our fellow man, making sure to copy their fashion while adding a twist of our own. Our best subjects of imitation were the ones we admired, our celebrities. If you go through history, past, present and most likely future, you'll see that we have always found ourselves going out of our way in our attempts to emulate our celebrities and their fashion. It's no secret that, even today, we are striving to dress like them and sometimes even admiring their fashion statements, and it wasn't any different in 1970. Considering how colorful those celebrities were I'm not surprised – but if there was one celebrity that undoubtedly stood above the rest, it was Jimi Hendrix.

Always dressed in unique attire, Jimi made sure to deliver a message through his fashion, leaving its mark on his own generation and the ones that followed. From the moment he took main stage and rose to fame, Jimi turned into an icon and a subject for admiration, but he was different. He simply didn't care his clothing made a fashion statement. Jimi's fashion had a more significant role in his life, it was a transmitter for something bigger, for the one thing that he loved the most – his music. Through his image, Jimi was able to serve his fans, delivering great music, but still how could anyone ignore his presence?

Have you ever browsed through Jimi's timeless photos? Check them out and see for yourself. There is no way to describe or ignore Jimi dressed in his vintage attire, his colorful vests and jackets combined with colorful bandanas and large hats with bright, violet ribbons. Yes, there was a lot of purple in Jimi's apparel. Interestingly enough, he was attracted to the color purple and always used it in his clothing. I wonder why.

Mark Twain once said *"the clothes make the man."* Well, in Jimi's case it was the opposite. Jimi wore clothing that already had meaning and redefined them, giving them whole new meaning. Doing so he was transformed into a style icon for decades to come, an object for imitation. But no one was able to replicate Jimi even after countless trips to the nearest thrift shop on a search for vintage or used articles of clothing. Jimi's fashion was an iconic representation of one person only and a symbol of the Seventies' unusual fashion.

Now why would I tell you all of that? How is this related to our purple aliens? Well, let's just say that, as the scouts before them, the aliens also began to associate with the seventies fashion. In a weird way, it was their only way to express themselves in a world that ignored their existence altogether. Their attraction to our fashion caught them off guard as they realized that it wasn't them who were conquering Earth, but Earth who was slowly conquering them. The aliens started to adapt to our way of life, and it was a revelation for them.

Since adaptation is a process that comes in stages, the aliens chose our fashion as their first step in that process. Their exposure to 1970's fashion worked magic on them, and it wasn't just the wide range of colorful clothing, but also the colorful band of humans who wore them. There was something else that ignited their souls, a new realization that came through their experiments with our fashion, something new they learned about themselves. They were introduced to a new kind of freedom, which made them liberated, discovering their ability to choose. For the first time in their lives, they were able to choose the clothing of their own liking and it was a huge discovery.

Those are the kind of things we take for granted, but for the aliens it was never like that. On their planet, they were all lookalike, identical purple entities, dressed in the same identical uniforms. They never knew any other way, which made them believe that they were the same, not just in their external appearance, but also in their personalities, their behavior, and set of beliefs. That was their way for thousands of years and they accepted it without question. They never imagined what it would be like to be an individual, to think and reason for yourself. They lived in the same quarters with the same furniture and the same purple-looking wives, always secure in their way of living and never knew any better. Among us, everything changed.

Dressed in human clothing, questions started to pop up. Who am I? What am I? What would I like to be? Their personalities started to emerge, and for the first time they became individuals with different opinions and perception of life. A radical change like that would never happen on their planet and for a good reason. How can something like that happen on a planet that for the last thousand years still argue about changing a single stich on their uniforms?

With their new finding, their minds opened and exposed them to our society and to the flood of ideas that came with it. From that point forward, nature took its course and was credited for all the other changes in the aliens' behavior. The aliens were now ready to adapt to any and all of our ways of life and I do mean any and all.

Some of them were instantly drawn to the free-spirited Hippies and wore their clothing, projecting the same views of freedom and love. They went head over heels for the Hippies' long bell-bottomed pants, loose clothing, and the tie-dyed T-shirts, unable to resist the use of a crown of flowers to complete their look. A crown made of daisies.

Others chose to express their solidarity with the disadvantaged Black Panthers and used their fashion to project their radical views, covering themselves with the Panthers' signature attire, the black denim pants, white T-shirts, black leather jackets, and black berets, expressing to the world their disappointment of whatever had disappointed them. You see, unlike the Black Panther members, those aliens never knew what disappointment and discrimination was but still had the urge to protest the feeling of disappointment and discrimination.

Let me tell you about my favorite ones. Those were the aliens who chose to dress as their idol, Jimi Hendrix. Being so impressed with him they did their best to imitate him, to no avail as Jimi was always in a league of his own. Still, it didn't deter them, but made them go further, adding special touches to their transformation in the form of an Afro wig. Dressed as Jimi and wearing a wig, they were close to a perfect transformation, but fell short on one small detail, Jimi's mustache. This is not a joke, but a sad reality. Aliens are just incapable of growing any facial hair - a well-known fact across the universe.

Those fashion statements reflected the differences between the two human groups. If there was one thing that bridged the gap it was that period's timeless music, played by groups and individuals who stepped directly into history while creating a segment in our pop culture, which is still parsed into our minds.

And one of them was Jimi Hendrix, who was able to deliver his deepest thoughts in great guitar licks that touched all of us, Black Panthers, Hippies, and the soldiers in Vietnam. Jimi's music was apropos of life, reminding us of the simple facts about ourselves, and through his music he taught us that no matter who we were, we were all the same, and that we all had the right to live the life of our choosing, to be happy in our choices, and not be judged by others.

If you think about it, during his glory years, between the late sixties and his passing in 1970, Jimi represented all of us in one person and one body. It is something that was reflected in his music, clothing, and attitude, telling us that Black, White, Radical, Hippie, Citizen or Soldier were all humans and had the right to express their personalities in the way they felt was right, just as he did. It was a very simple message that was accepted by all of us. We followed his words and went on our way to fulfill his vision as best we could. For once, we joined forces, protested and changed our country.

And, in fact, 1970 became a very busy year for us. We joined different movements and filled our lives with new routines. We had protests to arrange, gatherings to attend and wardrobes to worry about. Those functions were considered by us to be highly important, and delay of any kind, even of the third kind, was not an option.

But the invading aliens, who were now dressed in their new clothing, didn't know that. They continued stalking the rushing humans for weeks, tagging behind them, slowly realizing that they were not getting any closer to achieving their mission's goals. This tagging along got the aliens closer to us and our causes, slowly transforming them into active participants and full-fledged members of our movements. It moved them closer to our society.

The aliens started to align themselves with Earth's 1970 causes, making sure to get involved with the issues closest to their hearts. It was the beginning of a chain reaction, which became a major change in their objectives. They didn't abandon their original objectives, but just made them more provocative. You could still find them standing on street corners, subway stations or roaming the boulevards, still trying to convince passing humans to ignore their cute external characteristics and submit to their demands, but this time it came with a twist. They were doing so while holding a large protest sign in one claw, a joint in the other and smiling. Regardless, the results were the same – they were still ignored by us. How could they expect any other outcome, when everyone was so energized with the causes that, ultimately, changed our country forever?

It's a shame you couldn't have been there to see and feel it. Everywhere you went, on any major street corner, there were humans standing in small makeshift booths, doing their best to convince other humans passing by to sign their petition. Since the pushy booth organizers knew that the more signatures they collected the better chance their agenda had, they were willing to spend whatever time needed to convince any passers-by, human or alien, to sign. So one might say that the booth organizers closed their eyes and treated the aliens like the rest of the humans. The aliens got dragged into those booths, as the rest of the passing humans and were convinced to sign those petitions.

In retrospect, it seems that the aliens were an easy target for the booth organizers. Maybe it was their smiling faces or maybe it was their quest to feel like they belonged, but they signed these petitions with no reservations. In fact, it didn't take much for them to leave their mark on those petitions and leave those booths with a bigger smile on their faces. They left their mark for sure, a unique blue ink mark that resembled two sharp claws.

And the booth organizers? They didn't care much and ignored the countless strange and identical marks. For them those were additional signatures, a crucial proof of support, which amplified their voices and allowed them to be heard; but ironically, the aliens left something more than just an ink mark. By signing those petitions, the aliens left their mark on the same petitions that, later on, would change our lives so radically. For example, and as farfetched as it sounds, the same purple, smiling aliens who invaded our planet in a failed attempt to attack its population, played a major role in promoting the environmental movement's petition and establishing our planet's first ever "Earth Day."

This movement's goal was to establish a worldwide awareness with all people on the importance of our planet's environmental protection, to establish a day that would signify that cause, and that day was April 22, 1970. This day marked the height of this movement's push to promote their petition and collect signatures. To their luck, it just happened that the whole alien army, twenty thousand strong, was right there outside their booth. The aliens were dragged inside and signed this petition without question. There was no logical explanation for them to sign this petition, but sign it they did and in droves. By the end of that day and with the help of the aliens, April 22 was established as the official Earth Day, and is still celebrated today worldwide.

Years later, this historical petition was reviewed, not by an official committee but by a young student from an unknown, small community college who was working on a school project. Scrolling through the documents, the young student reached its last pages, the signature pages. To his amazement, he discovered a large number of them to be, for lack of better words, "out of this world." This finding piqued his curiosity and he started to dig deeper into the pages. Had he continued his investigation, it might have turned into a significant news item that would have altered the young student's life, bringing him fame and recognition – but unfortunately the young student couldn't resist his roommate's pleas to go out for drinks at the closest sports bar. By the next morning, and after a long night of drinking and a very bad hangover, the young student had forgotten about the whole thing.

One can only guess what went through the aliens' minds while signing this petition. Can it be that they were not aware of its nature or long-term effect? Was there any logical reason why the aliens would try to save the same planet they came to destroy?

Well let's just say that in a separate research of another petition, conducted by a young female student from another unknown, small community college, there were additional interesting findings. It was the 1970 "Women's Rights" petition that revealed the same amount of those odd signatures. The young student also wondered about the source of these strange signatures but since she was a great supporter of that petition herself, there was no other recourse than to leave that stone untouched. The two students, from those two unknown, small community colleges, never met and the dots were never connected, leaving that mystery unsolved. If they had ever met, they might also find out that on the same fateful day of April 22, 1970, the organizers of the "Women's Rights" petition had placed their booth on the same street, right across from the environmental group's booth. As I've told you before, the aliens were easy prey for the booth organizers and very easy to convince.

For us, it's simpler to believe they were clueless while signing the "Earth Day" petition and completely unaware of its goal to secure worldwide protection of our planet. Well, it's harder for us to accept that the aliens weren't as naïve as it seems. Maybe they were loftier than us, and in their short visit to our planet were able to recognize how special this place was, the place we call planet Earth.

We've been around this planet surface for so long, we take it at face value and nothing more. We, definitely, don't think much of it, believing that it will always be under our feet even while standing upside down in China. We have already established that between the hardships of our lives and the conflicts we are constantly getting involved in, humans are pretty busy. In fact, we are so busy we forget that our small blue and green planet is a very special place.

Did you know that it actually has a huge magnet at its core? Well, that's the same magnet that keeps our feet attached to its surface. Yes, I can see how you could forget this small detail. Still, it seems that unlike us, the invading aliens didn't. They couldn't resist their attraction to our planet's core.

Much credit can be given to our planet's core ability to attract the aliens, which led to the important occurrences of April 1970 and the two petitions' success, but it wasn't the planet alone. There was an additional component that contributed to the aliens' attraction to our planet.

It was the collage of the special humans of the late sixties and early seventies generation. For the aliens, they were an interesting group of humans that held an amazing spark for life, something the aliens had never experienced before. Maybe the aliens were lost on our planet, but they were still able to recognize our planet's multicultural society. They were counting on humanity's successes and defeats while developing appreciation for those who stood on the front lines.

Like the scouts before them, they were drawn into California's multicultural atmosphere and became comfortable in this new environment, reaching the point of defining their individual identities. In 1970 there was no better way to do so other than associating yourself with one of the humans' movements, becoming an active participant of those movements' functions.

If you are blessed with sharp vision, take a close look at photos from various demonstrations in California during 1970 and you might be able to see it for yourself. There is a very good chance that among the humans you'll be able to trace some very colorful smiling creatures, complete with small sharp teeth and beautifully manicured claws. Those are the aliens, the members of the great alien army, protesting and doing their best to voice themselves and find their place in our colorful society.

They wanted to prove themselves and became totally involved in our demonstrations, putting special emphasis on the anti-Vietnam war protests. They were standing with the humans, shoulder to shoulder, holding large makeshift signs in one claw while raising their other arm high in the air, making the famous V sign with their claws. You know which one? The same one that represents the peace sign. Well, at least it looked like it, but don't forget that the aliens had only two claws.

They were also easily spotted marching with the human rights groups protesting the current social injustice, demanding equal rights for all, including the rights of short and cute purple creatures. They were chanting and shouting with the rest of the demonstrators with the only difference that they were doing so in their native language. No one understood their slogans, but no one cared as they all appreciated the over-excited, funny-looking creatures' participation. The aliens were holding large, makeshift signs in one arm while raising their other arm up with the same familiar and famous peace sign, the V sign. Again, at least it looked like the peace sign as the aliens still had only two claws.

It might be that those activities gave them purpose or maybe it was just a way for them to spend their days, but their evenings were different. In the late hours of the afternoon, as dusk was setting, clearing the way for nighttime, the long day's excitement faded away. As the adrenalin-infused spirits of that day's protests were winding down, the aliens would retire with the rest of the protestors, in small groups, back to their communities.

Can you imagine that sight? Aliens and unsuspecting humans, sitting together and enjoying the best pastime activity of the sixties, the music. They would sit, until the late hours of the night, drifting away while listening to great music from those bands who came in the other invasion, the one that no one disputed as it definitely happened and remembered by all, the bands that came in the "British Invasion."

Every so often one of Jimi's songs would play and you could trace the immediate change in the aliens' facial expressions. Their pointy ears would stand up and a calm, easy feeling would come over their faces, making even this everlasting smile on their faces to subside. They gave his tune extra attention, even shushing any human who spoke while that song was playing. Their understanding of Jimi's music and lyrics was deeper than ours, and they were always on the lookout for hidden messages in his melody.

Soon after, as the music was playing vaguely in the background, the excitement faded and the conversations started. They would talk about that day's events and the struggles ahead, encouraging each other with positive hopes for a better future. The aliens would listen, quietly, to the conversing humans and on some occasions try to get involved, giving their two cents, but unfortunately for them and maybe for us, we couldn't understand them.

They had limited knowledge of the humans' language, and their attempts to emulate it made them sound as if they were mumbling. For the humans, the over-excited aliens seemed to be on a kind of a high, strong enough to impair their ability to speak, so it sounded like gibberish. And as we always do, we became impatient and lazy so we didn't make the effort to try and understand that mumbling, yet loyal, entities.

Looking back, I can see that ignoring their input was our biggest mistake. You see, we missed a golden opportunity to receive input from real outsiders, an objective source, and we gave it away. Since then and up to now, unfortunately, those kinds of objective opinions are no longer available to us. Instead, we've learned to accept opinions, which are not objective and always based on personal gain and hidden agendas.

Yes, we screwed it up big time, and we'll never know the wisdom hiding in the mumbling words of quirky, funny-looking short, purple, smiling creatures. Just think about it, what if they had the simple solution for all of our problems? What if they could give us a way to solve all our miseries? What if they had the answer for everything?

We'll never know...

At the very late hours of the night, the humans would retire to their quarters for highly required and well-deserved rest, getting ready for the new day ahead and its surprises. The aliens, on the other hand, would quietly retire as well but climb to the buildings' rooftops. There, they would lie on their backs and quietly stare at the stars of the night skies above them. Yes, stars in our big cities nightly skies. I know it sounds like a myth but in 1970 you could still see real, shiny stars in our skies, and I'm not referring to the ones on Hollywood boulevard sidewalks.

I can't tell you for sure what went through their minds while staring at the vast universe. Since they were used to roaming its galaxies, I do not know if they were still amazed by this endless creation. It might be that they were looking at the unbelievable view above them, trying to spot the same elusive, moving wormhole that started their adventure and which hopefully, one day, might lead them back home. Maybe they were trying to trace their far-away home only to realize that they couldn't see anything past the stars of our galaxy.

Or maybe they were just thinking about those damn, self-centered, lowlife pilots in the hovering spaceships in outer space who had left them to rot behind, with no care at all for the well-being of their comrades, the mighty and stranded alien army.

The aliens had a variety of experiences on our planet. Some were good and some not so much but all were shadowed by a single experience they endured during their stay on Earth, something they considered by far as the worst experience of their ordeal. It came in a form of a new feeling they never felt before, loneliness.

Far away from their home, ignored by their pilots, and completely alienated by the human society, they felt lonely. Incapable of connecting with human society is a gentle way to describe their interaction with us. It is more accurate to say that it was us who chose to ignore and ultimately reject the aliens and we didn't do it on purpose. We were just humans and did what we do best, overlooking whatever is in front of our faces, ignoring their existence. In this case it was the whole alien army, twenty thousand strong.

As much as the aliens did their best to get closer to the society they came to conquer, this society did everything they could to stay away from them. The aliens couldn't believe that at the end of the day, when all was said and done, they were nothing but a fun thing for the humans, a filler. There was no real camaraderie, no real friendship, there was only loneliness that was hard to overcome.

They couldn't comprehend how radical this change in their alien state of mind was, when loneliness crept in at the late hours of the night. All that feel good atmosphere they experienced during the day's events and all that brotherhood and togetherness accumulated during the evening gatherings would disappear in an instant with the humans' departure. Every night they found themselves staring at those night skies and each time they would sink a little more into that abyss of unknown feelings that we call loneliness.

And why would they feel any different? After all, it wasn't all peaches and cream on planet Earth. Not for the humans and, indirectly, not for the aliens either. How could it be good when the Vietnam War was still raging overseas? The aliens became aware of this human conflict through their participation in various demonstrations against the war. They couldn't understand the magnitude of this human conflict and not because they were never exposed to warfare. On the contrary, in their galaxy they had their fair share of conflicts with other alien nations, but those conflicts were different. Those were full-blown, intergalactic types of conflicts, which made the Vietnam War miniscule in comparison, but still there was one big difference.

In the aliens' view, Earth's conflict was primitive and cruel. It was a show of force that led to an end game of two sides trying to eliminate one another in the bloodiest way possible. They saw it as an ultimate attempt of a species to destroy ITS OWN SPECIES through blind and aggressive methods of destruction.

In their galaxy it was different, more "civilized," an organized event that was scheduled in advanced with a time and place agreeable to both sides. Normally, it would be on an isolated location, somewhere in the endless open horizons of the universe, in a distant place that wouldn't pose a threat to innocent lives or cause damage to ground structures. The two parties would approach each other at a slow pace, riding their largest and shiniest spaceships while engaging in some small talk, attempting to convince each other to lay down their weapons and go home while they still could. That in itself would be done in a melodramatic and respectful manner, and only if those talks turned fruitless would the two parties resort into action, starting with the dispatch of a large amount of small spacecraft that would perform extreme maneuvers, followed by cool metallic sound effects. Yes, there would only be a show of force that bears no casualties, an air show grade level performance that was the beginning part of the conflict.

If none of the parties gave up their positions a short time later the real showdown would start as the small crafts would engage with one another and create a scene that could only be described as the greatest and most colorful vision you've ever seen or imagined. Well, most likely you've never seen something like that as even our most talented Hollywood special effects personnel cannot replicate such a vision.

Let me try to describe it for you: Think about the most amazing computer game you've ever played, the kind that involves the latest visual effects available of flashing laser beams and incredibly colorful plasma explosions, now sharpen it ten folds and multiply its intensity in one hundred. Now clean the dust off your screen, and dim the lights in your room, and there you have it.

If you have never played computer games, try to imagine the best ever fireworks show you've seen in skies with no clouds, multiply it by one thousand and start blinking your eyes as fast as you can as you making sure to keep everyone around you is completely quiet and you'll get the same result.

It would be easier for you to forget this all fireworks show deal and get into the habit of playing computer games – you'll experience that vision much faster and simpler.

Now, if you've never played computer games or watched any fireworks show and don't care to get into the habit of playing computer games, well then it would be a good idea for you to work on your imagination or, at least, get out a little more.

Regardless, all that I'm trying to relay to you is that those visual features were of the utmost importance to the aliens. At first thought, it might come across as a showoff, but it wasn't. Those visual effects were capable to reduce the magnitude of any conflict before it would be blown out of proportion. In their world, there was always the hope that the mere sound and vision will convince either one of the parties to drop their shields and go home. If that didn't happen, at a bare minimum, those effects would transform any conflict, big or small, to a much prettier one.

In their world, even the worse of conflict would be resolved quickly with the two sides disembarking to their own territories with nothing gained and nothing lost, other than pride.

Since, hand-to-hand combat wasn't a common occurrence in an intergalactic alien conflict; there were no bloody scenes or carnage. The televised evening news showed footage of colorful plasma explosions and large bursts of laser ray beams, which, to the general alien population, made them seem cheerful. On the rare occasions where an alien's corpse was spotted floating in space, its slow, floating movement would also give the false illusion of calmness, but that was a very rare sight, since alien causalities would, normally, be decimated to dust at contact with those colorful laser beams and plasma explosions. That made the aliens' battlefields free of the kind of horror scenes you encounter in our bloody conflicts. As I've said before, unlike our conflicts, which can drag on for years and even decades, those intergalactic conflicts would reach a resolution by the end of the same day and the two parties would return home with only one thing in mind: How to clean the plasma explosion marks off their spaceships and bring them back to mint condition?

With this kind of logic, can you see how the aliens had it good? With all of their intergalactic conflicts, they were never, really, exposed to the pain and horror of a battlefield. Their exposure to Earth's bloody, painful and most of all messy conflict rattled them to the core. It dawned on them that the humans' pain and sorrow had no limits. It was able to pass the confines of the battlefield, cross oceans, and reach them at home. It grabbed their souls and squeezed without letting go.

The aliens developed their own ideas about our Vietnam War and even tried to share them with the humans. Maybe they had a peaceful solution for this lingering war or maybe they wanted to offer us the use of their laser guns and plasma explosions, the same ones they had waiting in outer space. After all, a few of those plasma explosions would most likely end the conflict in no time while transforming the bloody battlefield into a prettier, sterile one.

Whatever they had in mind didn't matter, since we were humans, who didn't care to listen, understand or even acknowledge them.

The aliens never witnessed the Vietnam War firsthand, but were exposed to it through the television footage, which came directly from that war zone on a nightly bases. They also witnessed the wounded soldiers returning to the ports of Los Angeles and San Francisco and didn't like it a bit. They assumed that being alien was an advantage as it allowed them, unlike the humans, to close their eyes in an attempt to stay as far away as they could from this painful conflict – believing that being on a visitor status would shield them from the conflict, but they were mistaken. You see, there is not a single war in which irony doesn't play a part. After all we go to war in order to do "good," so they say. That irony will give any war its own unexpected and crazy way to find you. Ironically, the Vietnam War found our purple aliens.

And this is how it went. You see, with the Vietnam War claiming lives on daily basis, there was a constant demand for new soldiers. The army needed new bodies to replace the fallen and in December, 1969, the government initiated "The Vietnam War Draft," which was introduced to American homes in the form of an official letter. That letter began with "Greetings from the President of The United States" giving you the sense that no good could follow. Well, it was the government's way to recruit young boys directly from high school and provide them, free of charge, with the army green attire and send them to a quick boot camp training, which by the army's definition turned them from boys into men.

Next, came the more complicated part of equipping those young men with assorted types of weapons and sending them abroad with one mission in mind: *"Meet new people and kill them."* The 1969 draft resulted in the complete alienation of those young soldiers from the population back home. Of course, that didn't stop the army from continuing the draft, which actually, was moving forward in full swing. After all, the demand for new soldiers wasn't diminishing but growing.

If there is one thing I can tell you about the United States Army in 1970, is that it was the one place you couldn't blame for being prejudiced. As it was drafting future soldiers, the Army didn't discriminate against anyone. It had an urgent need for new soldiers and would accept you as you were. It would take you regardless of your race, skin color, height or weight. Let's just say that the only color the Army really cared about was green, the color of its uniforms.

Most of our country's young men dreaded receiving that draft letter, but expected that sooner or later this personal invitation would show up in their mailboxes. So, one could say that for the humans, this letter was expected, but when the same official letter, the same personal invitation, started appearing in the aliens' mailboxes, it was completely unexpected and ironic.

How could an alien, a soldier of the honorable alien army, from a far, far away galaxy, be drafted into the United States Army?

How could the aliens join the same army they came to conquer? And most important, what would an alien who received such an official draft letter do?

Well, to the best of my knowledge most of them ignored it, taking it for an honest mistake, a typo by one of the recruiting officers – a huge typo. Some aliens folded it carefully and stashed it in their personal belongings as a memento from planet Earth. It was something to keep for their old age, when they would sit with their alien grandkids telling them war stories. What could be cooler than to pull out this letter at that exact moment and show off about the time they were almost recruited into the humans' army in a faraway galaxy?

Then there were some, not a lot, who took it one bold step further. They filled out the attached paperwork, accepting the invitation and sent it back to the draft board. Those aliens decided to join the United States Army.

I am sure that their decision to appear before the Army's draft board was based purely on curiosity. They promptly arrived at the recruiting center on their scheduled appointment date and found themselves standing for hours with the rest of the human recruits, the future soldiers, waiting for their name to be called, something easier said than done. They were watching the humans around them being processed quickly, unable to understand why their names were not being called as well.

The truth was that even if their names were called, they wouldn't know it. Since, they couldn't understand our strange language anyway. They waited for hours upon hours and only by a miracle, when they realized that no one was responding to the recruiting officer's calls, did they step into the room. They found themselves standing in front of the officers of the United States Army recruiting board.

That was where the fun began. Due to the language barrier, the aliens couldn't answer any of the recruiting officers' questions or, for that matter, complete the written test. The recruiting board wasn't willing to give up on any new recruit who was so persistent. With their best efforts, it wasn't long before they were left with no choice but to give up and reject the aliens. The aliens left the recruiting center with mixed emotions and an official rejection slip, which was covered with many big red stamps.

The big red stamps didn't indicate a specific reason for their rejection. The board itself couldn't put their finger on the exact reason. But there was a list of the board's recommendations for the aliens, something about solving their legal status in the country and also suggesting that they, immediately, enroll in ESL (English as Second Language) classes to improve their grasp of the language. The paper also instructed the aliens to reappear before the draft board in a year for reprocessing.

The board reassured the aliens not to be concerned about the end of the Vietnam War, promising them that it wasn't about to go away any time soon, and most definitely would be waiting for them in a year's time.

Those aliens, who by now had experienced much more than they bargained for, had no plans whatsoever to return. Not during their invasion planning or in their wildest dreams did the aliens imagine they would be able to gain access into one of the humans' military facilities without a fight, and leave it completely unnoticed.

The sad reality was that by now they were not surprised with any of the humans' conduct. They had already gotten used to the humans' complete disregard for their existence and could only assume it was the humans' way of ignoring anything and anyone who didn't directly impact their lives. They couldn't understand it but since they were stranded on our planet surface, with nowhere to go and not much to do, they decided to use our attitudes to their advantage. They started looking for a way to turn this situation into an opportunity, to establish a more fulfilling life on planet Earth, right under the humans' noses.

You see, during their forced stay on our planet, the aliens studied the humans' many ways of expressions, both verbal and non-verbal. Even as they regarded the humans as self-centered beings with a short attention span, the aliens learned to appreciate their many lifestyles and, to a degree, were consumed by their constant pursuit for individuality and equality. The aliens admired the humans' ability to pick a cause, nurture it like a newborn, and bring to fruition.

The aliens desired the same freedom of choice as enjoyed by the humans. Despite all of the humans' faults, they recognized the humans' vast knowledge on things they had never experienced. They knew that in order to obtain such knowledge, one must live among the humans. Their new desire wasn't due to the lack of freedom on their planet but for the lack of choices on their planet. Simply put, on their planet the aliens had nothing to choose from.

The truth was that their planet was pretty much a boring place, even visually. Everyone owned the same exact items, and due to their planet's zero gravity, there were no moving parts, it wasn't a choice, but a necessity. Everything had to be bolted to the planet's surface so it wouldn't float away and disappear into space. While comparing their grounded environment to Earth's loose and fast changing life, the aliens couldn't ignore a little nagging voice, in the back of their large heads, reminding them of the difference. They couldn't see themselves returning to a life where a dinner at a friend's house made you feel like you'd never left home as everything was identical, including him, his wife, their kids, and even their pet gronker.

Furthermore, because the aliens used hovercrafts they didn't need roads. There were never votes on new road projects, detours or pothole repairs as there were none - no choice here either. With no potholes, there were no speed limits, stop signs or any other road signs. Everything was, literally, up in the air.

There was no need for glass workers, moving companies or civil service employees, something that contributed to their high unemployment rate, but due to the lack of city employees –

nobody ever complained. Again it was a direct result of the lack of choices.

When it came to personal expression, one can say that it was non-existent. How can you express yourself with no choice of clothing? They were all dressed alike, same kind of uniform, same color - one size fits all. Maybe it wasn't such a big deal, but it was the perfect recipe for a very monotonous life, which showed the aliens how boring and pathetic their lives were. They felt even more pathetic, when it dawned on them that no one on their planet had ever owned a mirror.

Well, in all fairness, on their planet they never had the need for mirrors. Instead, they had an ancient method that was handed down from father to son for the last thousand years, a substitute solution. In their world, an alien on his way to a business meeting or a night out who had to make sure that he dressed to code would implement this method. He would knock on his neighbor's door and politely ask him to mimic his own movements and facial expressions. Since they all looked and dressed alike, this method worked flawlessly.

But now it was different. On our planet, they became individuals, wearing different clothing, looking different. Their ancient method wasn't working and the use of mirrors had become essential to their survival. Comparing their life to ours, the aliens thought themselves very lucky to encounter our way of life. You can say that they were thankful that, *"there WAS no place like home..."*

Knowing they were stuck on Earth for a while and maybe even for good, planted a crazy idea in some of the aliens' minds. They began considering Earth as their new and permanent home. They started to find a way to establish themselves on our planet, among us. And why not? After all, humans had no issue with them and if they did, they never show it. Those aliens went as far as considering opening small shops to cater the humans. They justified it as a good financial decision and great business opportunity. They asserted those small shops would be a good way for them to generate a steady source of income. Yes, it finally happened, our aliens couldn't escape our way of life and were a stone's throw from becoming fully committed capitalists.

They even had a flagship product in mind - candles. Not the ones you thinking of, but special kind of candles. The aliens, who came as drops, wanted to implement the same kind of drop process and manufacture candles from drops, "Aroma Tapered Candles" to be exact. They were already making those candles in their free time, in small quantities, and giving them away to their human acquaintances - so why not to make a profit?

During the sixties, those candles were a pretty groovy idea. They were colorful, psychedelic candles that you would attach to an empty bottle top. Light that candle and it would melt into colorful drops, sliding along the bottle sides, covering it with colorful melted wax, disappearing from the bottle top, making it available for the next candle.

The humans were mesmerized by those candles, staring at them for hours. It was something the aliens didn't miss and decided to exploit and profit in the process. In their excitement they overlooked one major factor that could work against them. The humans who were so mesmerized by those candles, were the same stoned Hippies that couldn't hold a conversation longer than two minutes. They were the ones who insisted that while staring at those candles they were able to travel to another dimension. They went as far as declaring those candles to be *"Groovy and Far Out."* Any businessman will tell you that *"Groovy and Far Out"* isn't the best measurement for long term financial success.

Let's just say that in 1970, basing your business success on the Hippies' financials wasn't a sound decision. The aliens had a great idea, but were heading to a disastrous execution. It was only pure luck that saved their behinds. Those business plans never came to fruition, maybe because there wasn't a single banker that was willing to loan them the initial business capital, or even a single shiny nickel after reviewing those plans. The aliens never opened those little candle shops and, unknowingly, saved themselves from inescapable financial ruin.

But it wasn't only the loan refusals that kept the aliens from starting a new, permanent life on our planet. There was also something much bigger, the ongoing Vietnam War.

It had a stronger effect on the aliens, much stronger than their exposure to our way of live, exposing them to the other side of our human nature, the darker side. It confused the aliens that the same part of our souls that enriched us could also embrace our endless pursuit for conflict, dictating that the bigger the conflict the more we were pleased. All the "Kum Ba Yah" feelings experienced by the aliens couldn't mask the war, the conflict overseas that was affecting the nation back home. It poured onto the streets of Los Angeles and San Francisco, creating a larger conflict on the home front. The aliens had an awakening and took a second look at our society.

It was another first for the aliens - the first time for them to understand the complexity of our society. We were not like them or any other alien nation they met before. We were not a single society, but a collection of different societies, each with its own sets of beliefs and all of those societies were encapsulated into a single race, the human race. It was the first time for them to understand how polarized we were and how we held our unbridgeable differences with our teeth, never giving an inch or compromise.

Now they could see more clearly how different were the Black Panthers from the Hippies and how both groups were further apart from the rest of us. Now for the first time, they realized how their supervisor's report, in which this invasion was based on, was wrong and misleading.

To say the least, that was very disconcerting for them, adding new question marks to the already stranded and lost aliens, something new to worry about. If the human society wasn't able to hold onto one set of beliefs and were so polarized from within, how would it affect simple purple beings like them? What may become of them after such long exposure to our planet and the humans on it? Would they be able to shield themselves from us and our behavior? Would there be long-term effects rising from this exposure? And the most important question of all: where in the hell were those damn pilots and what had we done to them to deserve such a communication silence?

The stranded aliens reached a crossroad and had to carefully choose their next step in this ordeal called "planet Earth's invasion." On one hand they still appreciated life on Earth with its opportunities and delights, which included close proximity to their idol, Jimi Hendrix. What could be cooler than attending his live shows at any given time with no need for advanced planning or a very long voyage to Earth from a faraway galaxy?

On the other hand, it came with a price – the almost sure and unpreventable change of their essence, which most likely would turn to the worse with their adoption of the human behavior. They were troubled by the slim chance of losing their personalities as they were facing ours. They had to make a decision if they were willing to pay that price.

Still dressed in humans' apparel, they were pondering their options, struggling to reach a decision. They were doing so while roaming the streets of the two large cities with no specific purpose, walking our streets in small groups, discussing their situation in their native tongue, trying to keep away from us, but still unable to ignore or pull away from any of the humans' public gatherings or protests they came across.

Every so often, they would wander into the same two neighborhoods that, three years earlier, served their scouts as the locations of first contact. I can't tell you if they reached those neighborhoods by chance or if it was done on purpose, but the aliens wouldn't miss the opportunity to drop in and say hello to those neighborhoods' residents. It was as if they had an unexplained, almost magical connection with the colorful residents of the Watts and Haight Ashbury neighborhoods, the same ones who had accepted both them and their scouts with open arms.

The lost aliens had the entire planet to explore or at least the entire cities of Los Angeles and San Francisco, but they felt more comfortable in the rough and tough Watts neighborhood and the laid-back Haight Ashbury District. In their current situation and considering all the hardships they went through, feeling welcomed was something they craved.

Their troubles started with their long journey to Earth followed by the much longer and frustrating drop process. They went through all of that only to find themselves lost without the generals and officers who had mysteriously disappeared, leaving them with no directions. If that wasn't enough, they were completely dumbstruck by their pilots' actions, their complete disregard and lack of support. The only thing they were left with was hope. They hoped that the large and shiny spaceships were still hovering in outer space and the day would come when they'd be back on those ships heading home.

All of that made them desperate, in need of a friend or at the bare minimum a hug. Next to Jimi, the residents of the two neighborhoods were the closest thing the aliens considered friends. They were the only groups who helped them. As usual, their "friends" were thrilled to see the aliens, but for all the wrong reasons. Their spirits were uplifted only because the aliens reminded them no matter how bad things were, there were those out there who had it worse than themselves.

The aliens would stay for a short visit doing whatever they could, with no success, to gain new information about the whereabouts of the desperately needed "Double AA" batteries. Then they would say their goodbyes and be on their way, aimlessly roaming the streets, pondering their situation.

Chapter 9 – The Evacuation

After weeks of walking our streets without direction, it happened. The aliens reached a decision to retreat from our planet, regardless of its opportunities, and return to their home planet. In their guts they knew it was the right decision. For sanity's sake, it was in their best interest to end this ongoing ordeal and leave our crazy planet. It was an excellent decision with only one small hitch - it wasn't that simple to fulfill.

You see, regardless of their decision, there were some obstacles that would affect the execution of their departure. Firstly, they had been unable to fulfill the invasion's most important objective, which was to locate and secure the highly desired and precious "Double AA" batteries. During their stay on Earth, the aliens hadn't succeeded in amassing a large stock of those batteries or for that matter even a single battery.

But above that there was a much bigger obstacle. They were stuck on our planet surface!!

The aliens had no way to transport themselves back to the large, shiny spaceships in outer space. They also had no means of communicating with their pilots in those large, shiny spaceships that were hovering in outer space. In other words, they were screwed.

It wasn't long before they realized it, but there was nothing they could do. They could only wait and hope for a sign of life from the spaceships, which hopefully were still up above, hovering in outer space.

Unknown to them, their pilots were now at the height of their game, completely immersed, and were not to be disturbed. The aliens were in a tough spot. Their only hope was that the pilots would eventually realize there had been no sign of life from the large alien army for the longest time. Maybe they would finally: connect the dots; understand something was wrong; and it might be a good idea to dispatch a search and rescue team to the planet's surface to hunt down the large alien army. A short time later, reality sunk back in and they accepted that nothing would happen right away. So they were left with no other choice but to continue roaming the streets of Los Angeles and San Francisco, without a purpose.

Call them lucky, but this time they didn't have to wait for long. It just happened that their pilots were wrapping up their long game, and to their credit, I must tell you that they were able to trace, with their little metallic eyes, all but five of the three hundred billion stars in our galaxy. Unable to trace the last five stars, the pilots agreed to end the game in a draw and look for another game, a harder one. While throwing out suggestions for new games, one of the pilots proposed counting the lights on the planet's surface below, starting with the beautiful green lights on the top of the globe, the ones that resembled an out of focus, green laser rays' light show.

The pilots looked through the spaceship's windows at the planet's surface below, considering their colleague's idea. As they were inspecting those lights and evaluating the game's difficulty, it dawned on them it had been a very long time since they had any contact from their army, the same one they had dropped a while ago on the blue and green planet below. That alarmed them and made them spring into action.

At first they checked their equipment and made sure that the long drop process had completed and there wasn't even one drop left behind. The confirmation that all of this time there wasn't one soul or one drop of their mighty army on the large spaceships hovering in outer space concerned them.

You would think that it was concern for their army's wellbeing, which made them take immediate action. Well, not quite. It was jealousy that overcame the pilots, who were certain that this communication silence was intentional on the part of the alien army. Most likely they were having the time of their lives on Earth's surface and had completely forgotten about their friends, the pilots, who were patiently waiting for so long in the large spaceships hovering in outer space. Only then did they attempt to contact the communication officers on Earth's surface with no success. There was no response, a complete radio silence, something that raised their irritation to an unprecedented level.

A short time after they came to their senses and started considering that there might be a valid reason for the radio silence. The pilots put their suspicions aside and decided to dispatch two small expedition teams to the planet's surface, one for each city. A few hours later, the expedition teams, equipped to the teeth, were on their way to Earth with a very specific order, to find the missing alien army.

By now, the pilots developed a real concern about their mighty army. What if something had gone terribly wrong with the drop process and their whole army, twenty thousand strong, was in a liquid form all over the planet surface? What if they had been able to go through that drop process, successfully, only to be wiped out by the crazy and unstable human society? And what if their mighty army was able to go through the drop process successfully, wasn't in a liquid form all over the planet surface, wasn't wiped out by the crazy and unstable human society, but was having such a good time on the planet surface that it had really forgotten about their friends, the pilots?

The last concern made them give very specific instructions to the expedition teams about the course of action they must take should they discover the missing aliens partying on Earth's surface. The teams were to contact the pilots immediately with the party's coordinates so they could join it as well. Upon arrival, they would party with their army for a short time, and only then the pilots and the expedition teams would return to the large, shiny spaceships hovering in outer space, start their engines, and ditch that selfish, large alien army for good. Since there was no time to waste, the expedition teams used small spacecraft to land at the familiar coordinates of the two neighborhoods. Upon landing, they hid their vessels and started a detailed search for their missing friends in the immediate area. It wasn't long before they found their comrades and what they unearthed rattled them to their core.

By now, what used to be known across the universe as the "Mighty Alien Army" was a mere shadow of itself. For the most part, they found them dressed with their colorful clothing and a lost look on their faces. The expedition team members who had never visited Earth or for that matter had never been exposed to humans were confused. They couldn't understand their friends' appearance, their clothing or the blank smiling expression on their faces. They went to work, attempting to piece together any information they were able to retrieve from the confused aliens. The more they listened, the more they became alarmed.

One thing was obvious. There were no parties on Earth's surface and no coordinates to send back to their pilots. The other most obvious fact was that this innocent blue and green planet wasn't as lucrative as it appeared to be from the distance of outer space and that immediate action was imperative. The expedition teams summarized their findings in a short and stern message, transmitted to the pilots, ending with three explanation marks. It was a simple message: *"We've found the army. Forget about the parties and for the sake of all of us, evacuate them off this damn planet - immediately!!!"*

Meanwhile, the lost aliens who witnessed the expedition teams' reaction to their sight heaved a sigh of relief. It only reaffirmed the uneasy feeling they had in their hearts about our planet. Now they could let their guards down and speak out loud what was never said before, labeling our planet for what it really was – a dangerous place. In their words, Earth was a harmful place and not just to them, but to its own population as well.

It was a serious situation that didn't pass lightly by the spaceships' pilots, who on their part moved immediately into action in an attempt to salvage whatever was left of their glorious army.

Never before in the history of this alien nation had it happened that someone deliberately broke the sealed glass that covered the red emergency button on the large spaceship's main console. This red button was their last resort, only to be used in case of extreme emergency. It raised the urgency level to its highest, cutting through any and all restrictions, giving the pilots direct access to their home planet. Pressing this red button allowed them to send an urgent message across any distance and any galaxy, back home. Most important, pressing this button allowed them to interrupt their commanding officer's, the supervisor, sleep at any given time, even if it was in the middle of the day, right after lunch, while he was in his office – "working".

The expedition teams' new revelations had to be shared as soon as *"alienly"* possible with the High Council and, of course, with the invasion's architect, our infamous supervisor.

The pilots required clearance to initiate an immediate evacuation of the alien army back to the large, shiny spaceships, still hovering in outer space. They gave him a detailed report of the alien army's "adventures" on our planet, which included specific details about the status of the invasion's objectives and most important, their army's declining mental and physical status. And there it was a small detail that raised a red flag with the supervisor, a very small and disturbing detail.

Now since you know our Supervisor better, what small detail could be so disturbing? Well, it wasn't about the alien army's slow drop process or the whereabouts of its top echelon that had literally disappeared from the face of the Earth. It wasn't even about the army's wasted time on our planet surface or their deteriorating state of mind. In his eyes, those were miniscule issues that could take a back seat. For him it was all about the unaccounted for replacement "Double AA" batteries.

He had just experienced a Deja-Vu. It seems that nothing has changed between 1967 and 1970, and like the scouts before them, the whole alien army, twenty thousand strong, was unable to put their claws on the desired "Double AA" batteries. As the scouts before them, the army's quest for the replacement batteries was a lost cause, impossible to fulfill, as if those batteries never existed. That wasn't the news he wanted to hear. The only sliver of good news he gathered was the aliens' accounts of their various encounters with Jimi. They were ecstatic and thankful for the rare opportunity to see him performing, stating there was nothing better than to see the man himself. They also pointed out that since it was very unlikely they would ever set foot on our planet's surface again they would greatly appreciate the supervisor's permission to see Jimi perform live one more time prior to their evacuation.

The supervisor absorbed the pilots' report carefully. Sitting alone, he gathered his thoughts, trying to figure out his next action. That became a light bulb moment that required one more meeting with the High Council elders. Only then he reestablished the communication channel with the pilots and gave them new instructions, commanding them to delay their army's evacuation until further notice. The alien army was not to be evacuated from our planet's surface before he conferred with the aliens' High Council.

And you know what that meant. Once again, our supervisor had to reach the High Council in their secluded space on the fifth floor of the main building in the aliens' Command and Control Center. Simply saying, once again, he had to pass through the building's friendly security team.

And he did. Right after he met the elders of the High Council to emphasize the crisis at hand. He told them about the invasion's current status and their army's unusual request, insisting it was one more sign that there was no better time to execute the "third secretive objective." He was short and direct, while convincing the elders to initiate the execution of that objective. By now they had to agree with him that it was the only way to solve the replacement batteries crisis.

Since their army couldn't leave our planet empty handed, the execution of his third and secretive objective was imperative.

It didn't take much convincing and by the end of their meeting, the High Council approved the execution of the "Third Secretive Objective."

Later, the Elders would justify their actions, saying they were in too deep with this invasion and had to agree. There were too many assets, resources, and time invested in this adventure, and since failure was not an option, they had to approve the supervisor's last objective. The aliens had to solve the replacement batteries issue once and for all.

Only then the supervisor left the secluded area and started calculating the moving parts of his objective, the two major components. First he had to find that special group of aliens, to execute this objective. They had to be exceptional aliens who could endure Earth's strange effects and roll with them. He already had a good idea where to find them and it wasn't far from where he was. Leaving the fifth floor's secluded area, the supervisor entered the staircase but instead of heading down to the first floor, he climbed one more staircase, to the building's next and last level – the roof.

As he guessed, they were just sitting there, colorful as ever, still smoking the same good old stuff they'd brought with them three years ago from planet Earth, still arguing the same old argument they had started on their way back. Yes, they were the original members of the aliens' 1967 mission to California, USA - the two scout teams.

Since their return, they were different, open-minded, thinking outside the box, and so were unable to see themselves integrating again into the aliens' society.

In their supervisor's eyes, this change wasn't good or bad. The scouts were harmless, but still different from the rest of the aliens. In fact, with their new personalities, they were a joy to be around and guests of honor at any party. But most importantly, they were the only aliens to survive our planet and return home with dignity. Since neither the supervisor nor the High Council knew how to deal with them, a decision was made to let them be as they were in their own secluded space, away from the rest of the aliens.

And what would be more secluded area than the space right above the very secluded area of the aliens' High Council?

They were left by themselves for a "just in case" moment and that moment as just arrived. The supervisor knew it was the right time to reassemble them. The original members of the 1967 scouting teams were the best aliens to perform this third, risky, and highly secretive objective.

The 1967 scouts were a special breed and for that reason, originally handpicked by the supervisor for the scouting mission. As long as one could ignore their childish arguments about senseless issues, one might say that their time on Earth had only improved them. After all, they were able to leave Earth after a yearlong mission and find their way home, while the whole alien army, twenty thousand strong, couldn't. Ignore their new weird behavior, their crazy colorful clothing, and their new-found love for the humans' contraband and you can say they hadn't changed a bit. Now they were about to be reactivated.

At first glimpse of their supervisor, the scouts, which were scattered across the rooftop, quickly gathered around him and greeted him with a cheerful hello and endless pats on his shoulder. Even though they knew he wouldn't visit them unless something was up, the scouts didn't forget their manners. Immediately, they offered him a rolled cigarette packed with some of the good stuff. They were surrounding him, waiting for him to speak. In return, the supervisor greeted them back, declined that highly intoxicating cigarette, massaged his aching shoulder and began speaking. After only few words, the scouts were already able to trace the tension in his voice.

To us, humans, it wouldn't sound like a tense speech, but as endless gibberish, spoken in a high pitch. It might be that we would be able to distinguish between regular, spoken gibberish and a nervous gibberish but even if we couldn't, most likely we could just pick out one or two words in this endless gibberish and those words were "Jimi" and "Hendrix", which were mentioned repeatedly in his speech.

Apparently, this very secretive third objective was very much connected with the aliens' idol, Jimi Hendrix. It seems that somehow the supervisor was able to establish a connection between the scouts' Earth mission in 1967, the aliens' futile pursuit of the replacement "Double AA" batteries and Jimi. Now was the time to exploit this strange link to the aliens' advantage in an attempt to revise the invasion's outcome.

The scouts were listening quietly as he was revealing to them his objective details and their role in it. The more they heard the higher their pointy ears stood up. Now they understood what made this objective so secretive, and why it had not been revealed in any of the invasion's earlier stages.

And there was a good reason for that. This objective was a complete contradiction of the first and most important rule in the *"Universal Multi Language Rules Guide Book."* The guidebook, which was as old as the universe itself, included contributions from almost every alien nation in existence. Since its main purpose was to maintain much needed order between all alien nations in the endless moving galaxies of our universe, it was considered by all as the universe's ultimate rule book. It was constructed as a collection of the universe's rules of conduct, adopted by all alien nations at the time of its creation, who swore to follow the rules. Those were important rules, painted in the colors of the galaxies.

For the most part, those rules were self-explanatory. But if there was one rule that above and beyond any other rule had to be followed, with no questions asked, it was the one etched onto the book's dark cover in metallic silver characters.

It was a very important rule that surprisingly and in a mysterious way was introduced to humans, in 1966 through the TV series "Star Trek," something they called *"The Prime*

Directive." The aliens' first and most important rule was a very simple one, stating that no alien nation would, directly or indirectly, get involved or alter the course of life of another alien nation, stating that such involvement might create a chain reaction that might alter the future of the whole universe forever. That was the way the rule was revealed to us through that television show. The way the aliens put it in the sentence etched on the cover of the *"Universal Multi Language Rules Guide Book"* was much shorter and direct. It simply stated:

"It's our life – Leave us alone!!!"

The supervisor's third objective wasn't just about to get dangerously close to violating this most important rule, but would drive straight through it. The scouts, like the High Council before them, realized that fact and were intensely listening. As he finished his briefing, they took some time to digest the new knowledge, trying to figure out their best course of action. The consequences of their failure in executing this objective would result in their nation's complete "alienation" by every other alien nation in the universe.

The supervisor sensed their thoughts, but insisted the reward was worth the risk. He even argued that being isolated wasn't such a big deal, unless they were planning to ever again take their vacation in the boiling hot, red beach, all inclusive resort located two galaxies away. There was no way for one to enjoy their stay when the local alien population gave you the stink eye, especially when each one of them was the proud owner of one hundred eyeballs.

There was a lot at stake and anyone else would most likely reject this request, but not the scouts. You see, they lived for adventure and enjoyed living on the edge, but also had a hidden agenda. They were running low on their stock of that good stuff and saw this mission as a godsend, a great opportunity for restocking. Regardless the reason, they chose to get onboard. I believe they summarized it with:

"What the hell, let's do it."

With their acceptance of the mission, the supervisor left the rooftop on his way to figure out the second piece of his objective's puzzle, the fastest and most important safest way to reach the invasion command center, the large spaceships still in orbit around Earth.

Then it happened once again. The supervisor was approached by the excited members of the aliens' scientific team, telling him that they had just finished the development of a new transportation method. This one could transport a full size, grown alien across any distance, even as far as planet Earth – at lightning speed. They swore by it, telling him this time they were able to find some aliens, dumb enough, to volunteer for testing the new method. This time the method was working. This time it was the real thing.

Still remembering the consequences of their original "drop method," the supervisor didn't care for their words and politely declined. His exact words were *"Buzz off."* Instead, he loaded the scouts on the aliens' fastest spaceship, slid into the pilot seat and left immediately toward our solar system and the large spaceships, orbiting planet Earth.

Using the spaceship's UPS (Universal Positioning System), he, finally, reached the small rock that was still spinning aimlessly around our planet and wondered how it could be that after all those years the humans were still unable to shoot this rock down. Getting closer to this rock, he traced a small, almost insignificant object on its surface, something that both surprised and terrified him. It was the same red, white, and blue emblem he had seen years before on the outside of the "Time Capsule," with the only difference that this was larger and mounted to a stick.

You see, in 1969 we landed on that small rock that was spinning aimlessly around our planet, the moon. Since we never pass the opportunity to show off, we made sure to leave our mark behind in the form of a flag that resembled that familiar emblem. It was red white and blue with some stripes and something that looked like stars that were drawn by an untalented four-year-old alien child.

Yes, I know that we've also left some tire marks, but I think that the flag was just a better way to let everyone else know who, exactly, left those tire marks!!

Since the supervisor always looked at the big picture, ignoring the little details, he became concerned. The humans' plan all along wasn't to shoot this small rock down, but to reach it and in his mind that meant that the humans had begun to exceed their boundaries. What if the humans considered going further into space? What if they decided to go beyond the limitation of their galaxy? What if they planned to reach other galaxies and maybe even onward to the aliens' home planet?

In his mind, the human society represented a clear danger, which made the immediate execution of his third objective a necessity.

The spaceship passed the moon, made a sharp right turn toward planet Earth, and the orbiting spaceships. It reached the largest spaceships, and right after their arrival, the supervisor and scouts situated themselves in their quarters and review the secretive third objective's details for the last time. A short time after, the scouts left the large spaceships on their way to the planet's surface.

And so it happened, on the first days of September, 1970, the scouts landed for the second time in California with a specific mission at hand – to find the whereabouts of Jimi Hendrix.

As expected, before starting their search, they made a detour to take care of some personal business; visiting the apartments they had left behind, watering their planets and making sure that everything was in order. Only then were they ready to start the search for their friend and idol, something that proved to be harder than they thought.

They started their search in the most obvious places, traveling up and down the California coast, only to find out that Jimi hadn't been around for a while. You see, in the beginning of

September, 1970 Jimi Hendrix wasn't in California or even the USA. He was in Europe, on the second leg of his *"The Cry for Love"* tour. The scouts missed him by just a few days, and there was nothing much they could do. After some discussion they decided that since it was an emergency, they wouldn't wait for his return but follow him to Europe.

Since they had never visited the European continent or encountered its population, the scouts decided to do their best to reach that continent while avoiding a new earthly ordeal at all cost. They wanted to reach Jimi without drawing extra attention from the humans. To do so they planned to rely on their previous experiences on Earth, although I'm not sure what part of their experiences they were referring to. They will use the humans' means of transportation while traveling to Jimi Hendrix's known last coordinates, leaving their spacecraft behind. Due to the time constrains, they rushed and acquired all necessary travel documents, visas and the ridiculously expensive last moment tickets.

Researching the colorful posters of Jimi's tour dates, they figured out that the best place to catch up with Jimi would be in the city of Fehmarn, Germany, Jimi's last and final stop of the tour. This show was scheduled for September 6, and there was no time to waste. The scouts crammed into a taxi on their way to the Los Angeles International Airport and boarded a transatlantic airplane on their way to Germany in their quest to find Jimi. They had to reach him just before his show, and be a part of what would later be known as Jimi Hendrix's last show of his last tour on Earth.

Can you imagine how complicated it was for a four and a half foot tall, funny-looking purple creature to pass through international airport security checkpoints and catch a transatlantic flight? How hard it was for the highly ticklish scouts to keep straight faces while being patted down by an airport security officer? And how difficult it was for them to ask a flight attendant, in midflight, for an additional small bag of peanuts - in German?

At least, they were smart enough to take the non-stop flight to Germany and not the one with the layover in France. After all, you know how short-tempered the French people are with someone who doesn't speak their language, and I am positive that even the aliens wouldn't have been able to handle the French attitude.

Be that as it may, by some miracle they were able to pull it off. Maybe it was because they stayed in their seats for the entire flight, and never asked for that additional bag of peanuts. No matter the reason, the scouts reached Germany and after some duty-free shopping in Hamburg International Airport, which included a German/English dictionary, they started their journey to the show venue. They only stopped once, in a small German pub, in order to taste some of that famous *"Schnapps"* they had heard so much about. To their surprise they found this alcoholic beverage helped them in handling the German language better than the useless dictionary. Now they could be on their way to catch up with Jimi.

It was a long drive but finally they reached the city of Fehmarn and drove directly to the show, the *"Open Air Love & Peace"* festival, where Jimi was about to close his European tour. It wasn't a scheduled visit, but since everyone in Jimi's crew recognized the colorful scouts, they granted them backstage access. Standing there, away from the crowd's sight, the scouts had one more golden opportunity to watch their good friend perform. They were witnessing his performance, listening to his voice and guitar, waiting for Jimi Hendrix to close his last show.

I wish you could have been there to see their faces and the mist in their eyes. I wish you could stand among them and feel the calmness that radiated from their bodies as they were drifting with his music to another dimension. Maybe they were overwhelmed by Jimi's exquisite performance or maybe they were sad that it was Jimi's tour finale or maybe, just maybe, they knew there was a much bigger finale on the horizon.

While on stage, Jimi caught a glimpse of the scouts. He was thrilled to see his short, funny, purple friends again and without a word, dedicated a song to them, *"Third Stone from the Sun,"* which he partly played with his teeth. Unfortunately, Jimi's action only ignited the scouts' same ageless argument all over again and they burst into vocal confrontation until they had to be shushed by the backstage crew.

When the show ended, Jimi walked off stage and greeted the scouts with warm hugs. He led them to his dressing room and shut the door behind. It was an unscheduled visit, behind closed doors, and even today its details remain a mystery. What made this short visit even stranger was that at its end the scouts left Germany and went straight to California faster than they flew in. Regardless of its details, one thing was clear, this visit produced an outcome that would affect both the aliens' and Jimi's future.

Upon their return to California the scouts boarded their spacecraft on their way back to the large spaceships, and the supervisor who'd been anxiously waiting for their return, biting the nails of his claws on both hands and feet. They wasted no time in briefing him with the details of their meeting, and as they were doing so, you could see a very large smile forming on his face. This time, it had nothing to do with Earth's gravity.

The supervisor immediately contacted the High Council, and soon after a final decision was formed, to begin the preparations for planet Earth's immediate evacuation, and that was an understatement. In a matter of two weeks, the aliens gathered all twenty thousand members of the alien army from the streets of the two cities, back to the secluded alleys and transport them to the large spaceships in outer space.

It might sound as a slow process, but with no city street maps or help from the eccentric local population, two weeks could be considered an achievement when you are collecting twenty thousand lost souls.

And so it happened that in the later part of September, 1970 the great alien army had vanished off the face of the Earth, leaving not one soul behind, not one trace or even single clue of their unexplained invasion or evacuation in the same invasion that never happened.

If you still doubting this invasion that in your mind, maybe never happened – then think about it as a simple question of observation and reality. Something like:

"If a tree falls in a forest and no one is around to hear it, does it make a sound?"

This is a question we understand and even happy to argue about. Well, it was just the same with the invasion that never happened.

The aliens did invade our planet, all twenty thousand of them. It just happened that we've never acknowledged them or their existence. Instead we made them feel unwelcomed, nonexistent, and lonely. The sad part was that they were not impressed by us either. The invaders who invaded our planet with aggression in mind didn't care for our aggression. They couldn't handle the dark side in us, the way we dealt with our own specie.

They just didn't like us and decided to leave, disappearing for good, without a trace. Does this mean they never been among us? That they never invaded? Does it mean that this invasion never happened?

But they did leave something behind. You see, during the evacuation process, most of them removed their colorful clothing and piled them in the back alleys, shedding what they considered as the last thing connecting them with the humans. It was as though they were trying to distance themselves from our culture. Only the diehard aliens who were dressed as Jimi Hendrix kept their attire on, including their Afro wigs.

I can't state for sure what drove the aliens to remove their clothing but I can tell you that soon after their departure, there was a new and unexplained phenomenon on the streets of San Francisco and Los Angeles. Suddenly, in both cities, you could trace a large amount of transients aimlessly walking around the cities' streets, wearing colorful clothing or black and white garb. The transients could easily be mistaken as the members of the Black Panthers or Hippie movements. Their only giveaway was that those transients never protested about anything.

How could they afford such clothing, you ask? Well, they couldn't and didn't have to. You see, those transients were the same ones who walked in the shadows of our society in the same secluded, back alleys that were formerly occupied by the aliens. As the aliens, they were also invisible to us and maybe even witnessed the aliens' evacuation and ignored it, but couldn't ignore the piles of clothing left behind for the taking. All that was left for them was to choose the clothing of their liking. It is true that the aliens' clothing was a little bit small in the shoulders and thighs, but we know that *"A **beggar** can't be a chooser."* The transients never complained.

Whatever happened in those back allies had no effect on us. It didn't change us. We were still the same kind of humans, who couldn't care less about our city's transients, no matter how they were dressed, the same way that we never paid any attention to the evacuating aliens and the clothing they left behind.

After two weeks the evacuation was completed and the soldiers of alien army were back on the large spaceships, which were still in orbit around planet Earth. They were very quiet, sitting in rows inside the spaceships' fuselage areas in a somber mood. Their minds were working overtime, trying to process the chain of events that had led to the rushed and unexpected evacuation. At the same time they were wondering of the long-term effects, their stay on Earth might produce, questioning if they have changed forever. Most of all they knew they had failed to fulfill their invasion's most important objective, to obtain a large stock of replacement "Double AA" batteries, and were overcome with disappointment.

They would no longer enjoy the sweet sound of Jimi's music. How could they? There was no other way to bring the humans' playing device back to life. There were no "Double AA" batteries. The only alternative they were left with came in the form of their horrible musicians who couldn't even get remotely close to Jimi's level. The mere thought they would have to listen to them for the rest of their lives, scared them and contributed to their declining mood.

After a second head count and confirmation that everyone were onboard, in their designated seats, the pilots fed the large flying machines' computers with new headings, put them in forward gear and began the long journey home. The aliens who were lucky enough to have window seats had their faces glued to the windows, as they couldn't resist getting a last glimpse of our planet. They watched the blue and green sight getting smaller and smaller, until it completely disappeared.

Only then, did they turn, looking straight ahead in total silence, like the rest of their comrades. Imagine those humongous spaceships at full capacity with aliens who were supposed to be ecstatic to return home, flying in complete silence. It was a dead silence. Twenty thousand aliens and not one word spoken even as the spaceships slowly left our solar system. The alien army was quiet – but it wasn't for long.

Out of nowhere, as the spaceships passed Uranus and were about to clear Neptune, there were loud cheers and the sound of laughter coming from the back section of the spaceship. The aliens in the forward sections couldn't ignore the joyful sound and turned around to find its source.

What they saw was the sight of their scouts who seemed to be in a good mood, laughing and joking with each other. It was a puzzling sight for the alien army. What could possibly make those weirdos so cheerful? Was it the result of the spaceship's high-speed flight? Could it be a direct result of all the "good stuff" the scouts were smoking? Or maybe those crazy scouts had, finally, lost their minds completely?

The spaceships left our solar system and continued on their journey. After a while they reached the same wormhole that had brought them to our galaxy. The pilots steered the spaceships directly into the wormhole's center and made the "Space Jump" toward their galaxy and home planet.

The long journey home gave the aliens enough time to adapt to their new reality and changed their gloomy mood into a happier one. They become talkative, greeting each other, happy to see old friends. After all, it wasn't all bad. They were going home after a long stay in a foreign land – and against all odds, they were alive.

At that point, everything fell into place. All of their adventures, experiences and misfortunes encapsulated in an instant into one great enlightenment. This Earth ordeal was an awakening experience for them, realizing they had to go through all of that, in a faraway galaxy and on an unfriendly planet, in order to learn something new about themselves.

Only then it dawned on them that regardless to their out-of-character conduct on our planet and no matter if they were radical or moderate, Hippie or Black Panther, happy or sad, they were at complete peace with themselves and most important, on their way home to their small, purple planet.

They were thrilled to recognize the planets in their colony's surroundings and completely jubilant when they caught first glimpse of their home. When the spaceships actually reached their planet and started the landing procedure, its bellies exploded into a huge roar. The aliens were giving "High Fives" to each other, or maybe we should call it "High Twos??" But not the supervisor. He had no time to waste, making his way to the spaceship's exit and practically jumping out of it as it was about to touch down on the planet surface. He was rushing, on his way to meet the High Council.

A short while after, he reached the familiar building with its friendly and smiling security team, but this time it was different. The supervisor had changed as well and this time he wouldn't let them have their way with him. He entered the building's lobby, bypassed the protesting security team members and pushed his way to the lobby's elevator, ignoring their protests. There were some urgent matters to take care of and there was no time to waste. Surprisingly, he found the elevators to be in working order. *"I guess those elevators were in working condition all along,"* he thought to himself, on his way to the fifth floor. He took a note of this as he swore to take care of those conniving security team members at a later time, once and for all.

He reached the High Council's secluded area, barged in, unannounced, and addressed the old aliens, describing his third objective's positive results. Emboldened by their smiles, the supervisor then switched gears. There were new issues to deal with, new concerns of high urgency, which had to be dealt with immediately.

What had suddenly become so urgent? What couldn't wait another moment? What had made the supervisor endanger his life, jumping off a landing large spaceship that almost crushed him? Well, sad to say, it was us – humans.

The supervisor had a genuine concern for any future contact, planned or not, between the aliens and our society. In his words, humans were an irresponsible society that posed a threat not just to themselves, not just to the aliens, but also to any other alien nation in the universe who might encounter them.

It was the time for him to admit what he'd done in manufacturing the misleading report and take responsibility for his actions. He saw the alarming signs about the 1967 returning scouts and ignored them. His only justification was that those changed-for-ever scouts were the best thing that had ever happened to the aliens. After all, they were the main reason for the successful execution of the third, secretive objective.

He told them the situation had worsened with his latest discovery of the same weird shape emblem on the moon's surface and the immanent danger of humans reaching their galaxy, but he had a solution.

In his eyes, since there was no reason for any future interaction with the human society, it was the time for extreme measures. As long as that roaming wormhole was out there, connecting their galaxy with ours, there would always be the threat of humans who might try to reach the aliens' world, and it wasn't the trying part that worried him as much as the succeeding part. That alone made it crucial for the aliens to protect their planet from any invasion, especially ones that might involve humans.

The aliens' questionable, recent experiences on Earth convinced the supervisor that any future encounters with the humans would be a bad idea. He told the elders that if it was up to him he would blow this wormhole to "Kingdom Come" or, at least, move it to another, remote part of the universe, where humans couldn't hurt any other life form.

He conveyed to the High Council tales about planet Earth's residents, those sweet talking humans who mislead you with slogans like *"We Come in Peace."* The way he saw it, this innocent sentence was only marking the beginning of the end for any alien nation who buy into it, including theirs. He described to them our endless need for conflicts, the main ingredient of our society's survival, and concluded that since the humans found it easy to concoct those conflicts on their home planet, on both national and international levels, there was nothing to deprive them of this golden opportunity to brew a new conflict on an inter-galactic level. He added that, most likely, we'll do so just for the hell of it.

By meeting's end, the Elders were convinced of the risks posed by the humans and moved into action with the release of a few urgent orders, starting with the immediate destruction of all and ANY items that had come in the humans' famous "Time

Capsule," including the precious Tape Player. They justified it in their fear from the remote possibility of hidden homing devices inside those items.

This decision to destroy the same device that had introduced Jimi Hendrix and his music to the aliens didn't go well with the rest of the aliens, even as deep inside they knew the risk and understood it was in their best interest. They had no choice but to follow the Elders' orders and with broken hearts threw the nonfunctioning, delicate device into the incinerator, watching it melt away.

Since destroying or moving the wormhole wasn't realistic, the elders resorted to an alternative solution, reflected in the posting of new large signs along the road, leading to the wormhole's entrance. Those weren't the type of advertisement signs you normally see on Earth's highways, but warning signs with the sole purpose of discouraging any alien, from any nation including their own, from reaching that wormhole and taking the road less traveled to the humans' galaxy.

The signs stated the danger ahead, attempting to deter ambitious aliens from starting a new adventure. The first sign was a presentation of a lovely young and smiling human family posing in a green park with the caption *"Slowdown Now!! Make a U-Turn ASAP!!"* The following signs were even more terrifying, having smiling humans in different social activities with slogans that gradually became more and more alarming.

The aliens could only hope those signs would discourage future, adventurous aliens from following their footsteps into the wormhole, but they weren't that dumb and knew there would always be an alien who would ignore the signs and reach the wormhole threshold. For that specific alien they constructed a very specific sign, the last sign. It was a humongous sign that almost covered the wormhole width, which they attached to the top portion of the wormhole entrance. This sign was meant to be direct in both image and slogan, showing our familiar yellow smiley face and pointing to a short and simple message, stating:

"So long and Goodbye. We'll Miss You – You Dumb Ass!!"

The aliens were just trying to do their best.

Chapter 10 – Jimi's Passing

Meanwhile, as all of that was happening in another galaxy, back on Earth came the bad news.

Jimi Hendrix was gone!!

The world lost Jimi on September 18, 1970. The musician, innovator, and greatest guitar player of all times was gone forever. Or was he?

Even today, after more than forty years, no one knows for sure the chain of events that led to Jimi's passing. There are still conspiracy theories and many open questions about the reasons and events that led to his premature departure. Regardless of all of that, the sad reality was that Jimi was no longer with us. Here on Earth, Jimi Hendrix was gone forever. We mourned that great loss and wondered if there was a way to fill the void inside us, the painful filling of losing someone close to you.

Jimi was a genuinely humbled human being, a soul that never hurt anyone, an artist who only cared for his creativity. He never cared for the greed and politics that surrounded him, but it did affect him and brought his spirit down. Still that shouldn't be the reason for him to leave us at such an early age, but when he was gone, his creativity and future contribution went with him. All that left behind was us, the ones who had the pleasure of enjoying his music and the misfortune to witness the emptiness.

During his short time on Earth, Jimi transformed into a cosmic being, made out of combination of physical existence and a strong spiritual component, a body and soul. And when he was gone, we felt as that something was missing and we were right. It was Jimi's soul that was missing, nowhere to be found.

We knew that Jimi Hendrix was gone, but couldn't say that he died. After all, even today you can easily spot Jimi's timeless images everywhere you look, whether on the cover of a magazine, between the aisles of any music store or in any clothing department. The same goes with Jimi's music, which is still playing on any respectful radio station.

We never lost Jimi. It just happened that his soul left his body and vanished from our materialistic human existence. It went off to another place – a more rewarding place that made more sense to Jimi. It is a place above our physical perception of life, a place that reflects Jimi's set of beliefs, where everyone, no matter who is just the same, equal. It is a place where maybe even everyone lookalike, think alike and dressed alike.

It might be even a place of eternity, the kind of place that allows Jimi to release his full range of creativity with no roadblocks, interferences or greed.

So, where did Jimi's soul go? Where is this place that encompasses all of those great qualities?

To answer this question, I must to take a step back and unveil some details about the supervisor's secretive third objective and the brilliant way it was conceived.

In retrospect, as complicated as this objective was, the third secretive objective didn't really contradict the universe's main rule of life. As a matter of fact it wasn't at all about altering or getting involved in our way of life. It, definitely, wasn't about distribution of alien technologies to the humans and as it turned out, it also wasn't about the aliens revealing their real identities to the clueless humans, who all along were unable to put their finger on the simple fact that there were aliens among them in the midst of the invasion that never happened.

It was about something else, which the supervisor was able to trace while combining the two completely, opposite, and polarizing scouting reports into the one he presented to the High Council.

It was a small and presumably insignificant detail he found on both reports, which he couldn't ignore as it was the only piece of information common to both reports. It was about Jimi Hendrix's perception of life. For no apparent reason, both scout teams found it necessary to include one of Jimi's quotes in their reports and that was the detail that caught our supervisor's attention. It was one of Jimi's simple quotes, a perception of life that, amazingly, aligned itself with the guidelines of the universe's number one and most important rule of life.

In Jimi Hendrix' eyes it was the simple belief of the way people were supposed to live their life and the same way he wanted to live his. He simply said, and I quote:

"I am the one that has to die when it's time for me to die, so let me live my life the way I want to."

And this is where I have to credit the supervisor. For the first time in his life, he was able to think outside the box and combine Jimi's desire to free himself from our planet's limitations with the aliens' ultimate goal, to have an unlimited access to Jimi's music at all time, for eternity. In his view, the roadblocks Jimi faced in his fight for individuality only made his decision to check out from our planet easier and in order to expend his being; he could use the aliens as the tools of execution. They would not intervene in his affairs and would never instruct him how to conduct his future. Jimi would be the only decision maker, the one to choose his path, releasing the aliens from any liability for his actions.

The secretive third objective's most difficult part was the creation of the right moment in which Jimi would reach his own decision. The aliens were hoping that Jimi would realize that there were places, other than Earth, which were more accommodating and limitless, places of another time and place.

After all, it was Jimi who hinted to the scouts to keep an empty seat on their return in 1970. That hint was the basis for the secretive third objective and when the supervisor received the army's request, to see Jimi performing one last time prior their evacuation, it only cemented this objective in his mind. In his eyes, it was a win-win situation and the ultimate solution for the replacement "Double AA" batteries.

You see, long before the invasion that never happened and right after the scouting mission, it dawned on the supervisor that since the batteries were the only means for the aliens to enjoy Jimi's music – a failure was unacceptable. In any circumstance, the alien army would not to exit planet Earth without replacement "Double AA" batteries. That made him formulate a plan where the aliens would engage Jimi one last time and for that he needed the scouts. After all, they were on a first name basis with Jimi and the only aliens crazy enough to take the leap of faith and engaged him. With the help of whatever they called "good stuff," the scouts would be able to reach different dimensions and maneuver around Jimi without revealing their ultimate goal. They were the only ones who could confirm if Jimi was still on board.

Was Jimi Hendrix really waiting for the aliens return? Had he finally decided to shed his human shell and join the aliens? Could it be that our most colorful and unique artist had better communication and interaction with those lookalike, think alike, dressed alike purple creatures from a very boring place, than with his own society? In all fairness, I believe that he did.

Remember that on their planet, there wasn't even one alien. On their planet they were all normal and equal entities. Can it be so absurd that Jimi's thoughts and aspirations were better understood by the aliens, the ones who didn't even speak his language?

All the supervisor had to do was to read between the lines. Everything stacked up in favor of this one chance that Jimi would accommodate the aliens and leave with them. That was the secretive third objective's ultimate goal and the scouts had to execute it with caution. Ultimately, the wish to depart had to come from Jimi's mouth, without any proposition from them. They could have led him through, but were not to put words in his mouth.

Since I don't know for sure, I can only speculate that the aliens were successful in executing their secretive, third objective. And to clarify even more, I have to take you back to Germany, to the place of Jimi's last performance on Earth and the unscheduled secret meeting the aliens had with Jimi, just before his passing.

This meeting's details are still shrouded with mystery and since the time of the invasion never happened to date, there wasn't a single human who could explain why, following this meeting, the aliens left Earth in such a hurry?

And I did try to ask some people that same question, only to be faced with questions like: What? Aliens? On Earth? Invading in 1970? Have you lost your mind?

Well, it does appear that the supervisor's secretive third objective was so secretive that no one even heard about it. At least, there is not one human on Earth who was aware of it. More than that, it was so secretive that excluding the supervisor and the scouts, no one else in the entire alien army, twenty thousand strong, knew about it or its successful outcome. None of the aliens who were sitting inside the large spaceships, in a quiet and somber mood on their way back home, paid any attention to this one quiet and somewhat lonely alien. He was sitting alone in the far right corner of the large spaceship's belly and could be easily mistaken to be one of the die-hard aliens who refused to disrobe. Still wearing his colorful clothing, afro wig and dark sunglass, he looked just like them and just like the rest of them, he kept to himself and never left his designated seat.

But unknown to them, he was different. A closer look would reveal that all along, behind the dark sunglasses, he kept his eyes closed as he was concentrating on perfecting something during the long flight. His claws could be his giveaway as he was playing an imaginary guitar and never stopped playing, perfecting his tunes for the rest of the trip to the aliens' home planet.

Could it be Jimi Hendrix in another form? Was this a part of the supervisor's plan? Did Jimi's soul fly free with the aliens to their home planet? Was this the outcome of the secretive third objective?

If the answer to all those questions is YES, then it was something that would only happened with Jimi's consent, something that had been discussed between Jimi and the scouts in 1967, during their first encounter, and became a more viable option in 1970, during their last encounter, at the time of the invasion that never happened.

One can only assume that during their last encounter in Germany, Jimi reached the final decision to seal the deal.

It was during this unscheduled secret meeting, when the scouts executed the secretive third objective. The plan was simple. For the first time, the scouts revealed to Jimi the story of the "Time Capsule," the moving wormhole, the "Double AA" drained batteries and their endless quest for replacement ones. Obviously, as usual they added their own twist to the delicate objective and remembered to mention their desperate need of a new stock of the same "good stuff."

All along they made sure not to suggest, beg or advise Jimi of his future decision. They described in detail all the hardships their army went through in its attempt to resolve the batteries situation – but never mentioned their final objective. They emphasized their current dilemma and told him they had to evacuate their army as soon as possible, but couldn't leave our planet without a solution for those tiny yet elusive devices. They made sure to stay within the supervisor's secretive third objective's guidelines and executed it without revealing its ultimate goal.

They finished telling their tale and became quiet, waiting for Jimi's response, which caught them by surprise. Jimi started laughing uncontrollably. Now he understood the nature of that weird present the scouts had given him three years earlier, the two drained "Double AA" batteries. He laughed so hard that the stage manager stuck his head into the room to make sure that everything was OK.

When his laugh subsided, Jimi sat the scouts down, took a long breath and explained to them how simple it was to acquire any kind of battery, in any size or quantity, in any convenience store or supermarket. That made the scouts blush with embarrassment. How stupid could they and the entire twenty thousand members of the alien army have been? How can it be that none of them ever thought to enter any of those establishments and buy a four pack of "Double AA" batteries?

When Jimi saw the scouts' embarrassment, he calmed them down and said: *"Have no worries, brothers, it's not a big deal and can happen to anyone. I think I have a better idea."*

That made the scouts to hold their breath, raise their pointy, and wait for Jimi's next words...

Jimi told them that the purchase of additional batteries would only serve as a temporary solution, which would force them to make additional trips to Earth for restocking purposes, something that could not be economically justified.

In my belief, that was the moment when Jimi spelled out the words the scouts were waiting for, telling them that the best solution to their problem would be if he would leave with them.

"Think about it." He said, *"If I go with you, you'll never have to return to Earth ever again, not for batteries and not for that good stuff, you love so much."* He smiled and said: *"After all, I can show you how to grow it..."*

I believe that Jimi had already made up his mind, trusting it would be best for him to exit planet Earth with the aliens.

You see, by 1970, Jimi was tired by all the white noise around him, the way the humans conducted their affairs. He felt as if he had served Earth's creatures as best as he could and that it was time for a change, the time for him to move on.

And when he was gone, he made sure to leave some clues behind, hints of his whereabouts. Today, you can read it in Jimi's own words, which are etched in a single floor tile in the center of Jimi Hendrix's *"Sky Church,"* located in the "Experience Music Project" museum in Seattle, Washington and it says:

"to be transported to another time and place."

That was Jimi in his own words (you can Google them), telling us of his wishes to leave to another place, completely detached from our earthly perception of time and place.

For those, among you, who don't know, young readers – the "Experience Music Project" museum is conveniently located beside Seattle's world famous *"Space Needle"* structure that from one unexplained reason shaped like a flying saucer, go figure...

He knew that it was his time to go and now he had the means of transportation in the form of those huge spaceships orbiting in outer space that were owned by short, funny-looking, purple creatures who loved him so much.

It might sound odd, but by the end of their meeting it was Jimi who did all the convincing, trying to reassure the scouts that it was his decision and the best solution for the replacement "Double AA" batteries problem.

The scouts made a perfect score. They were able to execute the secretive third objective, achieving its goal without compromising the Universe's primary rule of life and without jeopardizing their nation's standing in that universe.

Now they could relax, so they leaned back and watched Jimi as he stretched his arm toward his personal luggage, put his hand inside and took out a small, colorful, and delicate box. Jimi gently opened the box and exposed its content to the scouts. There inside were the two drained batteries, the same ones given to him by them a few years earlier. The scouts became emotional, realizing Jimi had kept his promise, to carry those batteries with him at all times. They continued observing him, taking off his iconic black hat and removing the bright violet ribbon off it. Jimi sliced two small, equal pieces of the ribbon and wrapped each piece around one of the drained batteries, finishing it with a neat bowknot. Only then, Jimi handed the scouts the two wrapped batteries and said:

"I have kept my promise to you out of friendship and respect. It is time for you to do the same for your fallen friends, the ones you've lost."

He simply asked them to return to the two places that were so significant to them on Earth, the Watts Towers monument in Los Angeles and the famous street sign at the corner of Haight and Ashbury streets in San Francisco. He told them to put one of the wrapped drained batteries in each location as a symbol of respect and commemoration of their fallen, lost friends. You see, for a brief part of his life Jimi was a soldier and regardless his feelings about the Vietnam War and any other act of violence, he understood the importance of respect for your brothers in arms, especially those who had paid the ultimate price.

For the aliens, it was something new, they never experienced before, to respect your fellow lost and fallen aliens? In their world, they never cared about the lost and fallen ones as there never were any; usually they would just get obliterated. But it was

Jimi's request and they promised to fulfill it, telling him that upon their return to California they would follow his wishes and pay respect to their two top generals, four communication officers, the entire translation team, and countless alien foot soldiers that had vanished without a trace.

If you ever find yourself standing in front of the Watts Towers monument, located in the Watts neighborhood of Los Angeles, or leaning against the famous street sign at the corner of Haight and Ashbury streets in San Francisco, there is a good chance that you'll be able to find an expired drained "Double AA" battery wrapped in a bright violet ribbon, finished with a neat bowknot. That would be one of the two batteries that had been left behind by the aliens. If you find that battery, maybe then you'll finally be convinced that the invasion that never happened – actually did happen!!

Always remember that those two batteries are no longer the typical *"Made in California, USA - Double AA batteries,"* but very special ones. Those are the only "Double AA" batteries, I'm aware of that were able to leave our planet, reach a faraway galaxy occupied by short, purple aliens, and then return to our planet in one piece. What made those batteries even more special was that those are the only Earthly items I've encountered that had been touched not once, but twice by an un-Earthly entities, once by the aliens and the second time by Jimi Hendrix.

Considering that those batteries are more than forty years old, most likely they have lost their shine and the bright violet ribbon has lost its luster. But those batteries are still there, serving their purpose, respecting the lost and fallen ones. Just go and see for yourself and if you are already there, there is one more thing that you can do.

You can keep those batteries' shine and the violet ribbons bright. You can continue the chain and keep the aliens' promise to Jimi Hendrix alive. You respect the ones who paid the ultimate price.

Just do a simple thing. Bring with you a "Double AA" battery, preferably *"Made in California, USA"* (if you can still find one that is not "Made in China"), wrap it in a bright violet ribbon, finished with a neat bowknot, and gently lay it in one of the two places that were so important to our aliens. After all, those were the places that were so accommodating not just to the aliens but also to the two very polarized and important groups in the shaping of our history, the Black Panthers and Hippies.

Is there a better way to respect the lost and fallen? These simple "Double AA" batteries commemorate those who have gone forever in different conflicts and places during the years that passed form the time of the invasion that never happened. And I do mean both humans and aliens.

We'll never know for sure the conversation Jimi had with the scouts in his dressing room on September 6, 1970, at his last show of his last tour on Earth. If you ask me, I am almost certain it went like this:

Alien Scouts: Was Ist Los, Jimi? (It's German for: What's Up, Jimi? in English).

Jimi: What's Shaking, My good purple friends? (It's English for: Was ist Shaking, My gute purple Freunde? in German)

Alien Scouts: Not much, overcoming the jetlag and this German schnapps, you had a rocking show tonight.

Jimi: Yeah Man, full house. What are you doing here? Is it time already?

Alien Scouts: We are good to go home, waiting for your decision. Are we cool?

Jimi: Here man, oops sorry, here purple alien, smoke this, chill out.

Alien Scouts: the Spaceships are waiting; we'd hope to leave in one week or maybe two max. Hey bro, this stuff is rocking!!

Jimi: Rock on. Did you hear me playing "Third Stone from the Sun," our song? Wow, it was good to be on Earth for a while.

Alien Scouts: Yeah man, it was good and now it's done. Are you on board for an intergalactic ride?

Jimi: Yeah man, Earth became too small. Let's say, in two weeks in London? You do know where my flat is?

Alien Scouts: Far out. Give us your address before we leave. Now where are all the groupies we've heard about?

The scouts stayed with Jimi until the early morning hours, having deep conversations about life itself, the choices it presented, and the cosmic effects of those choices. On his part Jimi was able to solve, once and for all, the scouts' endless argument, showing them the way he played his guitar with his teeth. Unfortunately, I can't give you more detailed information. After all, he demonstrated it behind closed doors. Knowing both Jimi and the scouts, I know it was a meaningful night as both were introduced to new aspects of life.

At morning's first light, the scouts left Germany on their way to California, to update the supervisor with their success. In return to their actions, their pilots received the very much anticipated "Go Ahead" command, to commence the alien army's evacuation and as we say here on Earth: *"The rest is history."*

Well, since this invasion never happened it is not a part of our history, it's nowhere to be found in our history books, but it did fill a whole bookshelf in the aliens' historical records building.

When the evacuated members of the alien army were sitting inside the large spaceships, they were clueless of what had transpired in Germany, two weeks prior to their evacuation. They never knew about the third secretive objective and its execution by the scouts. In their minds, California/USA/Earth's invasion was a complete and utter failure. They were leaving empty-handed, never aware that in their spaceship's belly was one of planet

Earth's greatest musical treasures. That was why they couldn't understand the scouts' cheerful mood aboard the departing spaceships.

Only as the spaceships touchdown on their planet surface and shutdown their engines, the secret was revealed. Only then, they and the rest of their colony realized how blessed they were to have Jimi Hendrix among them. It was as if they were able to breathe again. More importantly, now they were able to kick down the locked door of the sealed soundproof room, where their best musicians were still playing dreadful music, attempting to imitate Jimi and shut them down for good. The musician couldn't be more grateful.

In a matter of seconds, all of their worries had just vanished into thin air as they knew Jimi Hendrix wasn't going anywhere. He was there with them to stay until the end of time.

Yes, Jimi would live and play forever and still is. If you don't believe me, check this out: In 2013, more than forty years after his departure from our Earthly life, a new album was released with twelve of his tunes, we've never heard before. It called: "People, Hell and Angels."

Here on Earth, they told us those songs were pre-recorded before Jimi's passing. I guess – but not sure if the world will never know.

Chapter 11 – The Aftermath

This could be the end of my story about the invasion that never happened. After all, in the aliens' eyes, there couldn't be a better ending. What is better than having the ability to listen to Jimi's divine music with no worries of drained batteries or crazy humans? But this is not the end of my tale. There was something else that happened.

The aliens' encounter with our planet and its inhabitants produced another outcome, a positive one. It made the aliens gain a new appreciation for their monotonous way of life on that small, boring, purple planet. Placing those warning signs on the road leading to the wormhole, allowed them to take a step backward and start concentrating on improving their future. With their new addition, in the form of the colorful and talented Jimi Hendrix, there were no longer concerns about replacement batteries and they were able to invest their time in enhancing and protecting their lives on that small and precious purple planet.

With their new knowledge about us, the aliens had a valid concern about their future and it wasn't just their lives they were concerned about, but the lives of any other alien nation in the universe. As a result they sprang into action. They had to make sure that the *"Human"* threat would be known in every corner of the universe and with any existing alien nation in it. So they summarized their Earth ordeals into a publication, which they distributed across the universe, in every galaxy and in every alien nation, including the four alien nations who had actually lived in the four corners of the universe.

The publication started with a sensational headline, the same kind you find on our gossip magazines' front pages, which had been introduced to the aliens during their stay on our planet. It was written in the aliens' language in big red letters and it spelled out:

"BEWARE!!! HUMANS ARE NOT A MYTH!!"

The publication told the sad story of our society. It described a society that is pondering, on daily basis, the meaning of life and the ways to improve it – only to get further and further from the answer with each passing day.

It was a story about a divided society, made out of beings of different social background, status, and even color that took overt pleasure in pointing out one another's shortcomings, a society that never tried or wanted to help or solve their fellow man's misfortunes and failures. The publication ended with a stern warning to the rest of the alien nations, recommending that for their own safety it would be best to avoid the human society at all costs!!

Ironically, this publication was distributed on material, which very much resembled our earthly paper. Amusing as it sounds, apparently the aliens were quite impressed with this 1970 humans' form of communication. Since they were suckers for any new things, it wasn't long before it became their new obsession.

And I am not surprised as this new obsession had a good explanation and an indirect connection to their idol, Jimi Hendrix.

You see, in 1970 we had no computers, internet, email or social networking. Paper was the main form of social networking, a fact that wasn't ignored by the aliens. While on Earth, they realized that in order to trace Jimi's whereabouts, they had to follow his colorful tour posters, which were glued on buildings and fences on every street corner of Los Angeles and San Francisco. Since they found those posters to be so informative and reliable, they considered the posters and the paper they were printed on as an advanced form of communication, a kind they had never encountered before. Right then and there, the aliens vowed that upon their return to their home planet, they would implement this mind-blowing method of communication - go figure.

And they did, at least for a few years, until the true nature of this advanced form of communications was revealed, that is, its downside. It took only a few years for new mountains of discarded paper to form and cover large areas on their purple planet. It was a problem of such magnitude that it had to be dealt with immediately and decisively.

And it was - the aliens did solve their problem by blowing those new paper mountains into space with their largest plasma gun, creating a whole new galaxy, in the process. It was a very colorful galaxy, full of stars and planets made out of colorful discarded paper. Parallel to that, the aliens abandoned this advanced Earth technology and resolve to their old method of communication, telepathy.

In any case, their publication was a success and made large waves across the universe, resonating with every other alien nation, planting fear in their hearts. Its impression was so deep that it was recorded as the first and only time when all alien nations, without argument, were able to reach a new resolution. And when I say all alien nations, I do mean that it also included the alien nations who for millions of years couldn't come to agreement about the color of the red planet.

They all met in an undisclosed location, unknown to the humans, and agreed to revise their maps and charts, marking planet Earth as a danger zone, a place to avoid. The space between Earth and the moon became a "No Fly Zone," the aliens new "Bermuda Triangle," a place you always try to avoid, but always seemed to get in your way, a place you'd rather detour around than drive through.

Their decision to include the moon in the danger zone was based on the supervisor's observation of that red, blue, and white emblem on a stick on its surface. He convinced the other alien nations that since the humans were able to reach the moon there was no other choice but to mark it as one of the universe's most contaminated places, second only to Earth.

Being able to reach an agreement, the nations moved to create a new emergency procedure for any alien who, somehow, found itself stranded on our planet surface. I don't have this procedure on hand or know its exact details, but know it called for a decoy rubber doll, four and a half feet tall with greyish smooth skin, large head and two big triangle-shaped metallic black eyes.

The procedure instructed the stranded alien that:

"In case of increased human activity in your immediate area, make sure to leave this decoy doll behind for the humans to find. Then, proceed and make your way off this planet immediately. Make sure to launch straight up from where ever you are without looking back or stopping for at least five minutes."

The decoy doll's color and general shape were based on writings the aliens found in the humans' Si-Fi novels. I guess that while roaming our streets aimlessly, the aliens finally used some of that free time to visit our small book stores and read those famous Sci-Fi novels, getting a better idea of our expectations while encountering aliens.

For your general knowledge, this decoy doll color and general shape was as far as can be from any existing living alien across our universe, but the rest of the humans would never know.

But it didn't stop there. Since they all agreed to stay away from Earth and its society, they further agreed that it would be a good idea to observe us from afar, like lab rats, monitoring our technological advancements, making sure that the genie or maybe the devil would never leave the bottle.

They signed all the necessary documents, notarized them with the official universal seal and stapled them to the back of the *"Universal Multi Language Rules Guide Book."*

After billions of year in existence, this small stapled paper, which described the agreed interaction of any existing alien nation in the universe with us, the human race, became this book first ever amendment.

Only then were the alien nations able to return to their daily disagreements of one of the universe's ultimate paradoxes: *"If a supernova occurred while there is no alien around, does it make any sound?"*

While I'm sure they are still arguing over this timeless paradox, I know they stood behind their agreement. In fact, since September, 1970 and up to date, right after the aliens posted the new warning signs and with the implementation of the new rules of engagement, there has been a major reduction in UFO sightings by humans.

We, on the other hand, have never stopped looking at Earth's skies, never giving up the search for UFOs, never quitting our search of new life forms and there is no wonder why. You see, life on Earth can become boring and we'll do anything to acquire a new toy to play with. We'll look everywhere for a new friend that might stop for a short visit and hopefully leave some shiny new gadgets behind.

But the aliens are doing a very good job in avoiding us and since there is nothing in sight, we let our imagination run wild. We fantasizing, creating imaginary friends, just like any lonely child do, claiming to see them when no one is around. In some extreme cases, we even declared to be abducted by them, asserting they mistreated us and even performed surgeries on us.

News Flash: Aliens have no interest in us whatsoever!!!

Now, that doesn't mean that our planet is no longer visited by aliens. Here and there some adventurous alien youngsters will take their parent's spaceship, without permission, I might add, and go on a joyride. Since youngsters always know it all, they will ignore their elders' orders and be attracted to the forbidden wormhole entrance and this danger zone called planet Earth. It won't be long before they will hop on the highway, on their way to the wormhole entrance, making sure to leave a trail of aliens' graffiti on the aliens' new warning signs. They will reach the moving wormhole and with no second thought align their spaceship nose with its center, not without forgetting to post their most outrages marking on the humongous last sign above it. Now they were ready to be on their way to a new adventure.

They would enter the wormhole only to come out on its other side on their way to Earth, making sure to make a hard right turn as they pass the moon. They would land on our planet and realize they didn't charge the spaceship's power plant prior to their departure. Now, they were stuck on our planet's surface, waiting for their spaceship's power plant to re-charge. They would wait for hours, doing their best to avoid any human contact, hoping to disappear into space at first morning light, but never forgetting to leave large, weird-looking crop circles behind.

One might think it was the youngsters' rebellious mind that made them create such complicated geometrical designs, but that's not exactly true. Those circles are a direct result of a very bored group of young aliens who had nothing else to do while waiting for hours for their parents' spaceship to re-charge.

On some occasions, the absent-minded young aliens would leave behind a little bit more than just weird-looking large crop circles, things we consider as aliens' technology or more accurate young alien's technology. Those are the same cool, shiny, and slick little gadgets, you find in our high-tech markets. They are very appalling to any youngster even a human youngsters, turning them, instantly, into an absent-minded ones. If you have a teenager at home you can see the effect, they always forget something behind. Up to now, however, there has been no official confirmation or denial from any source for those allegations and all we are left with is speculation.

Those were the rare occasions when we had visitors from outer space, but overall, the aliens understood the danger and kept themselves away from the humans and their scrutiny of space.

Years have passed and peace restored on Earth and the universe. The Vietnam War has ended and our soldiers returned home. Humans were able to return to their daily activities, which were mainly composed of looking for new conflicts, but it wasn't the case with our purple aliens. Unlike us, they gave up on their aggression and adopted a more harmonious way of life as conflicts were the furthest thing on their mind.

And why would they look for new conflicts? They had no reason to do so. After all, they had one of the most peace loving entities in the universe with them. They had Jimi Hendrix.

There is no way to confirm if it was only Jimi's music or the man himself who on September 18, 1970 left Earth with the aliens, the day that marked the end of the aliens' invasion that never happened. No matter which it is, the aliens had Jimi.

Since there were so many stories of Jimi's belief in aliens and their existence, it wouldn't be a surprise if he did depart with the aliens to their home planet. Those are the kind of stories we can only wonder about, but there is one thing I am sure about.

At night, when the sun just ended its shift, and the night skies are taking over, that's when things become more interesting, fascinating.

If you don't believe me, take a few minutes of your busy daily schedule and no matter where you are, lie down on your back and stare up at those night skies. Hopefully, you'll be lucky enough to see a bright, shiny falling star, moving across our planet skies. That would be the right moment for you to close your eyes, relax your senses and listen, really, really carefully.

It might just happen and you will hear one of Jimi Hendrix's tunes softly playing in the far distance.

Well, those are the aliens, passing by our planet, disguising themselves as a bright, shiny falling star, as they are still doing their best to avoid us, humans - the real aliens in this vast universe.